D1625044

Friendship means
so much to you
dear Victoria.
Thanks for
including me
as your friend.
I love you

To My friend, Victoria

May this year

and years following

be the best

ever for you.

Presented to:

Victoria

My love,

Alma

FROM

Christmas

OCCASION

Dec. 25, 2000

DATE

FOCUS ON THE FAMILY®
presents

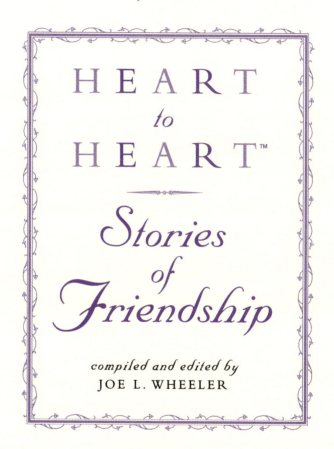

HEART *to* HEART™

Stories *of* Friendship

compiled and edited by
JOE L. WHEELER

TYNDALE HOUSE PUBLISHERS, INC.
WHEATON, ILLINOIS

Visit Tyndale's exciting Website at www.tyndale.com

Copyright © 1999 by Joe L . Wheeler. All rights reserved.

A Focus on the Family book published by Tyndale House Publishers, Inc.

This text or portions thereof are not to be reproduced without the written consent of the
editor/compiler.

Woodcut illustrations are from the library of Joe L . Wheeler.

Heart to Heart is a trademark of Tyndale House Publishers, Inc.

Designed by Jenny Destree

Published in association with the literary agency of Alive Communications, Inc., 1465 Kelly Johnson
Blvd., Suite 320, Colorado Springs, CO 80920.

The Apocrypha quotation is taken from *The New American Bible*. Copyright © 1970, 1986 by the Con-
fraternity of Christian Doctrine, Washington, D.C.

Library of Congress Cataloging-in-Publication Data

Focus on the family : heart to heart stories of friendship / compiled and edited by Joe L . Wheeler.
    p.   cm.
  ISBN 0-8423-0586-6
  1. Friendship—Fiction.   2. Short stories, American.   I. Wheeler, Joe L ., date
PS648.F72F63   1999
813'.0108353—DC21   98-53875

Printed in the United States of America

05   04   03   02   01   00
7   6   5   4   3   2

In Memoriam

Dr. Walter C. Utt
of Pacific Union College

My bridge from adolescence into adulthood,
my mentor and friend, who is mourned by all
of us who were warmed by the sun of his
presence and by his lifelong love for us.

(Further tribute in "I Can See Him")

CONTENTS

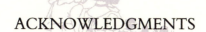

ACKNOWLEDGMENTS

"Introduction: The Many Roads to Friendship" by Joseph Leininger Wheeler. Copyright © 1998. Printed by permission of the author.

"The Mail on Corridor Three" by Winifred Kirkland. Published in *The Youth's Instructor,* September 19, 1916. Text used by permission of Review and Herald Publishing, Hagerstown, Maryland.

"The Stranger Who Taught Magic" by Arthur Gordon. Included in *A Touch of Wonder,* Fleming H. Revell, 1974. Reprinted by permission of the author.

"The Third Ingredient" by O. Henry (William Sydney Porter). Included in *Options,* Doubleday, 1909.

"First Honors" by Richard Marden. Published in *The Youth's Instructor,* February 7, 1928. Reprinted by permission of Review and Herald Publishing, Hagerstown, Maryland.

"The Tail of the Lobo" by Penny Porter. Reprinted courtesy of *Arizona Republic.*

"The Rebirth of Tony" by Sherman Rogers. If anyone can provide information on the earliest publication and date of this old story, please relay information to Joe L. Wheeler, c/o Author Relations, Tyndale House Publishers, Inc., P.O. Box 80, Wheaton, IL, 60189-0080.

"A Woman to Warm Your Heart By" by Dorothy Walworth. Originally published by the *Baltimore Sun,* March 5, 1944, and condensed by *Reader's Digest,* April 1944. Reprinted courtesy of the *Baltimore Sun* and with permission of Reader's Digest Association, Inc.

"Pinky" by Mabel Leaton. Published in *The Youth's Instructor,* May 8, 1928. Reprinted by permission of Review and Herald Publishing, Hagerstown, Maryland.

"Thank You, Rosie" by Arthur A. Milward. Reprinted with permission from the January 1980 *Reader's Digest* and from the author.

"A Darling" by Ernest Gilmore. Published in *The Youth's Instructor,* January 20, 1914. Text used by permission of Review and Herald Publishing, Hagerstown, Maryland.

"Blue Ribbon." Author and original source unknown. If anyone can provide information on the origin of this old story, please relay information to Joe L. Wheeler, c/o Author Relations, Tyndale House Publishers, Inc., P.O. Box 80, Wheaton, IL, 60189-0080.

"Whath Yo Name?" by Carolyn Rathbun-Sutton. Published in Review and Herald's *Insight,* July 9, 1988; in *Insight's Most Unforgettable Stories,* 1990; and in *Journey to Joy,* 1997. Reprinted by permission of Review and Herald Publishing, Hagerstown, Maryland, and the author.

"The Girl at the Telephone." Author unknown. Published in an old issue (date unknown) of *The Youth's Instructor.* Text used by permission of Review and Herald Publishing, Hagerstown, Maryland.

"My Eyes with a Waggin' Tail" by Joseph Tolve Jr. Published in *Life and Health* magazine, August 1973. Reprinted by permission of Review and Herald Publishing, Hagerstown, Maryland.

"Her Best Work" by Howe Benning. Published in *The Youth's Instructor,* December 15, 1914. Text used by permission of Review and Herald Publishing, Hagerstown, Maryland.

"One More Prayer" by Ronald Boyd. Published in *The Youth's Instructor,* October 6, 1942. Reprinted by permission of Review and Herald Publishing, Hagerstown, Maryland.

"The Lame Duck" by Thomas A. Curry. Published in *The St. Nicholas Magazine,* February 1927. Copyright not renewed.

"Dementia Praecox" by Della Dimmitt. Published in *The Youth's Instructor,* September 21, 1926. Reprinted by permission of Review and Herald Publishing, Hagerstown, Maryland.

"Table Service." Author unknown. Published in *Sunshine Magazine,* March 1939. Reprinted by permission of Garth Henrichs, publisher of Sunshine Publications, Litchfield, Illinois.

"When Muddy Creek Overflowed" by Harriet Lummis Smith. Published in *The Youth's Instructor,* April 30, 1929. Reprinted by permission of Review and Herald Publishing, Hagerstown, Maryland.

"Framework" by Josephine DeFord Terrill. Published in *The Youth's Instructor,* April 30, 1934. Reprinted by permission of Review and Herald Publishing, Hagerstown, Maryland.

"Silas Peterman's Investment" by Susan Huffner Martin. Published in *The Youth's Instructor,* March 1, 1927. Reprinted by permission of Review and Herald Publishing, Hagerstown, Maryland.

"I Can See Him" by Joseph Leininger Wheeler. Copyright © 1998. Printed by permission of the author.

THE MANY ROADS
TO FRIENDSHIP

Joseph Leininger Wheeler

I set out to find a friend,
but couldn't find one;
I set out to be a friend,
and friends were everywhere."

(*Sunshine Magazine,* June 1976)

ne of my most memorable epiphanies occurred a number of years ago at a national convention. As I walked toward a small group of milling people, inwardly I was thinking: *I wonder what they think of me? Will they like me? Is my tie straight? Is my hair combed neatly? What will I say if someone speaks to me? Will anyone recognize me?*

Then it hit me. Why was I worrying about all this? Weren't these the same questions each of them was asking? They weren't thinking about me at all—they were wondering what *I* thought of *them!*

It is upon this innate need for appreciation that friendship is based. Most of us perceive it backwards, assuming that all we have to do is tell everyone how wonderful we are, and the world will be ours. Strangely enough, the more we attempt to convince, the more resistance develops against us. It is the same principle of human perversity Socrates and Aristotle capitalized on: *Tell me how wonderful you are, and I'll battle to the end of the world in order to prove you aren't; tell me how inadequate or wrong you must be, and I'll battle just as fiercely to prove you worthy of adulation.* Odd, isn't it, how so few of us have capitalized on this great principle of human behavior.

Christ spoke about it more than once, declaring that the self-anointed chief at the head of the table would be removed to make room for the humble one who chose the least conspicuous seat at the other end.

Once I forever put aside self, the world will begin to open up to me. Once I become enthralled by the life stories of others, others will become interested in my own.

All we have to do is ask those leading questions: "Where are you from?" "What kind of work are you in?" "My, that's a beautiful painting! Did you paint it?" "What a great cook you are!

There must be quite a story behind your culinary genius; would you mind sharing it with me?" The list of openings is endless, but the results are all the same: The sweetest song in the world for each of us is the Story of Self—never, though it play forever, do we tire of that melody. And anyone who appears sincerely interested in hearing it . . . is a probable friend.

It is that simple.

Well, let me qualify that a bit: It is far simpler to make a friend than to keep a friend. I may spend a lifetime developing a friendship . . . and lose it in seconds. A friendship can never be taken for granted—certainly not the strongest and dearest friendships of life. They must be kept up, and any deterioration must be repaired as soon as possible.

Let's digress for a moment and consider the myriad ways friendships come into our lives. First of all, there are our parents. For most of our early years they are authority figures rather than friends, but if a parent has the courage to trade in the adult/child relationship for a lateral friendship as the child reaches young adulthood, a strong friendship can continue growing throughout their lifetimes.

Next, let's take siblings. In all too many families, siblings grow up antagonists rather than friends. That was unfortunately true of my brother Romayne and me. Not until we were both adults did we really become close friends. But if siblings are able to graduate from siblinghood to friendship, this relationship has the potential for evolving into one of the strongest life can bring.

Next to sibling relationships in duration and intensity are relationships with grandparents. Grandparents often become the dearest and deepest friends we will ever know. Perhaps because they are *not* authority figures, they become our friends much earlier than our parents do. And we must not forget uncles and aunts; and their children, our cousins—our extended family. Oftentimes these relatives become surrogate parents and siblings. Just as is true of our grandparents, uncles and aunts tend to turn into friends and mentors very early on. Not surprisingly, these friendships with uncles and aunts tend to become extremely strong, and the friendships with their children, our cousins, tend to develop over our lifetime (because of parallel longevity) into some of the strongest friendships of our twilight years.

Nor should we forget those nonbiological "uncles" and "aunts" most of us grow up with, not discovering until much later that they are merely *honorary* relatives. These individuals, along with godparents, often turn out to be among our most trea- sured mentors as well as friends.

Also among the strongest friends and mentors in our lives are likely to be certain teachers. Our teachers represent the bridge out of childhood dependency to adult self-sufficiency. Supremely blessed are we if we are mentored by a great teacher, one who refuses to take undue advantage of our admiration or hero wor- ship, but pursues a course geared instead to our long-term success.

Sometimes ministers enter into our lives through their words, acts, and interest in us. Because we often tend to idealize our spiritual shepherds, even cameo friendships often result in lifelong impact, completely disproportionate to the length of time the relationship lasted. More often than not, the minister will not even be aware of the impact of what was said.

Then there are the friends we make in elementary school, high school, and college. These tend to be among the most lasting of all our friendships. Such relationships are forged when our pas- sions are intense, our attitudes toward everything are in a state of flux, and we are far more open and vulnerable than we will ever permit ourselves to be again. Because we spend so much time with them and because we have few adult-type distractions to pull us away, the memories we jointly make are extremely vivid. My wife and I just returned from her high school class's fortieth-year reunion. What never ceases to amaze me is how irrelevant time is with these friendships forged so many years ago. They all pick up where they left off ten, twenty-five, forty years before. It is wonderful! Especially is this true of friendships made in school dormitories, as ours were. Intriguing is the fact that such friends tend to perceive you more as what you *once were* than what you have *since become*.

Now that we have dealt with friendships made during our growing-up years, it's time to turn to the adult counterparts. Of these, first and foremost would naturally be one's husband or wife. In addition, some of the strongest friendships of our lives are forged in the workplace. Then we have the friendships developed outside the home in activities related to church, community-involvement groups, sports, hobbies, humanitarian causes, etc. Because each of these involves getting together with people who love the same things we do, the odds are exceedingly high that deep friendships will result. In fact, out of this group are likely to come soul brothers and soul sisters who may dramatically enrich our lives.

We also make friends during periods of uprooting, danger, or trauma. Because these relationships are forged in the crucible of pain, anxiety, or even the likelihood of imminent death, they are likely to remain significant even though many years may pass without contact. If you doubt this, just listen when a group of wartime buddies get together. They will instantly forget *everyone* else, even close family members, as they interact with these individuals who were once central to their lives. The intensity of these friendships remains for life.

Then there are pets. Over time, some of them become closer and more dear to us than many of our human friends. I know people who refuse to travel unless they can take their pets with them. Because pets' love is unconditional, when they die it's like losing a member of the immediate family.

We must not forget our vicarious friends—and these are unique in that rarely will we know them as individuals. Perhaps it is a favorite composer, artist, or author. While we will never know these persons face-to-face, they nonetheless may have a significant impact on our lives.

Last and most significant of all is friendship with God. Think of David's day-by-day friendship with his Lord as seen through the psalms. All the great men and women of faith have treasured God as their dearest and closest friend. In a more contemporary setting, think of that wonderful drama *Fiddler on the Roof* and the protagonist's moment-to-moment dialogue with the Eternal. Speaking personally, my communion with God is rarely formal, but it *is* constant: "Lord, I've messed up again . . . please help me to do better next time." "Lord, I've misplaced my appointment book. Can You please show me where it is?" "Lord, this story has come to a dead end; if it is Your will that it be written, You will have to take it from here."

A MANY SPLENDORED THING

As we have seen, our friendships are as varied and complex as life itself. Now that we have considered the many roads by which friendship comes to us, it is time to address the heart of the matter: What is friendship, and what is God's role in it?

At the very beginning of Genesis, God declared, "It is not good that the man should be alone," and He created Eve. God programmed us to be social beings, to be interdependent. Significant indeed is the worst threat hanging over the world's criminals—worse than death itself to many—solitary confinement. To be cut off from humanity, one's friends, is to die.

In *Mere Christianity,* C. S. Lewis discusses God and relationships:

> If you could see humanity spread out in time, as God sees it, it would not look like a lot of separate things dotted about. It would look like one single growing thing—rather like a very complicated tree. Every individual would appear connected with every other. And not only that. Individuals are not really separate from God any more than from one another. Every man, woman, and child all over the world is feeling and breathing at this moment, only because God, so to speak, is "keeping him going." (New York: Macmillan, 1943, 156)

All interconnected. Nothing, no one, is ever alone in this universe. In a faculty week of prayer a number of years ago, I spoke on "God's Incredible Choreography." I likened God to a Grand Master chess player, to whom this world is one vast chessboard. He plays us all together, yet individually, on this cosmic chessboard. Again and again in my own life I have experienced God's split-second timing, such as when He took me off one train (stopped by a flood), flew me to another, and positioned me across the aisle from a woman who desperately needed what God impressed upon me to share. Before we retired (in the wee hours of the next morning), wiping away tears, she declared, "God put you on this train!" If we are will-ing, God will use us in marvelous ways, as conduits of His grace, to those we meet each day. To each of these we may come as a friend, and during our interactions, short or long, we may be privileged to introduce that greater Friend, and in so doing, change that person's life forever.

C. S. Lewis gave a lot of thought to the role of friendship. I believe his book *The Four Loves* is the greatest book ever writ-ten on friendship. One section radically changed my perception of what friendship is. Lewis hypothesizes that there are three almost inseparable friends: *A, B,* and *C.* They are always together. Suddenly *B* dies. Now *A* has more of *C* and *C* has more of *A.* Not so! declares Lewis. Now *A* has *less* of *C* and *C* has *less* of *A!* The reason? Because there was something in *B* that unlocked part of *A* and part of *C* that no other human being will ever be able to duplicate. In truth, each of our friends unlocks a different door into our heart, mind, and soul; and when a friend dies, a door will remain locked shut as long as we live.

After I read that, for the first time I understood how parents, when another child is born, do not divide their love among the other children. *Each child brings its own supply of love with him or her.* I also better understood why old people are often so lonely. As each of their friends dies, one of the survivor's doors is locked. The cumulative effect gradually reduces the size of the world that person lives and interacts in. Only one thing can reverse that fatal inversion: continuing to make new friends as long as we live! Perceived in this way, we quickly realize that friendship repre-sents God's way of expanding our potential: Each new friend—or each deeper relationship with an old friend—broadens our vision, deepens our insights.

Dr. Frederic Loomis, in his book *The Bond Between Us,* postulates that friendship itself represents another dimension in life. He suggests that Person A represents one dimension, Person B another, and the bridge by which they reach across space to each other represents a third dimension: a force that could never exist had the two personalities failed to interact, a channel born of the impact two lives have on each other.

FINAL THOUGHTS

As we near the end of this brief journey into friendship, let's note a number of things about friendships:

- Friendships cannot be taken for granted, not even the strongest ones. Upkeep is essential if they are to flourish. Our technological society affords many ways to retain friends when distance precludes personal interaction, such as phone calls, faxes, E-mail (more and more common), and the old-fashioned personal letter (typed or handwritten). Sadly, many of us are physically removed from some of those we love most, so we must establish alternative methods of communication if we are not to lose their friendship. Some of the most meaningful and treasured relationships of my life have resulted from personal letters.
- Friendships cannot flourish without an element of mutual respect. Oddly enough, not even criminal relationships can outlast loss of respect.
- Beware the power of words! Many friendships have been lost because of loose lips. Sometimes the words are forgiven—but they are never forgotten! "Friends are made by many acts—and lost by one" (*Sunshine Magazine,* February 1958).

- A true friend will risk even the relationship itself rather than see the other hurt. How well I remember stepping in once when a friend was needlessly putting her reputation at risk. The immediate result was a noticeable cooling of our friendship, but the long-term result was that this friend is today one of the closest friends I have. Through the experience she learned that her personal success in life was more important to me than the friendship itself—and there can be no stronger friendship in life than one based on such mutual trust. Other friends have done the same for me.
- Few friendships can survive repeated acts of borrowing, for damage is likely to occur on both ends rather than one. The same is true for involving friends in business deals—I learned *that* particular lesson the hard way!
- Only in adversity do we learn who our true friends really are. It is said that a friend is the person who walks in when the rest of the world is walking out.
- A true friend brings out the best in us. Unquestionably, we become like our friends. We can achieve honor and respect by our choice of friends, or we can lose both honor and respect by the wrong choice.
- Never has it been said better than Joseph Addison did: "Friendship doubles joy and divides grief."
- Treasure most your old friends, those who have stood the test of time: "Forsake not an old friend; for the new is not comparable to him: a new friend is as new wine; when it is old, thou shalt drink it with pleasure" (Sirach 9:10)

In conclusion, friendships can thus range from momentary meetings lasting only minutes to lifelong relationships. Each relationship we have gives back to us in proportion to what we give. Quite probably, friendship represents God's greatest earthly gift to us. Multidimensional and multihued, friendship represents the difference between a wasteland and an Eden in our day-to-day lives.

Truly, friendship is a many splendored thing!

MY DREAM

It is my earnest hope that this collection of stories, along with the other books in this series, will enable you and your family to begin building a large collection of wonderful old stories. Stories that convey strong Judeo-Christian values; stories that are virtually impossible to put down once we start reading them. Stories that, when their values are internalized, will result in the kind of character we want our children to grow up with. And to those of us who are a little older, these stories will remind us of what life, the Christian walk, and our daily ministry to those around us are all about.

CODA

Each reader of this collection is invited to help us compile additional volumes by searching out other stories of equal power, stories that move the reader deeply, stories that illustrate the values this nation was founded upon. Many of these stories will be old, but others may be new. Please send me copies of the ones that have meant the most to you and your family. Include the author, publisher, and date of first publication, if at all possible. With your help, we will be able to put together additional collections centered on other topics. You may reach me by writing to:

Joe L . Wheeler, Ph.D.
c/o Author Relations
Tyndale House Publishers, Inc.
P.O. Box 80
Wheaton, IL 60189-0080

May the Lord bless and guide the ministry of these stories in your home.

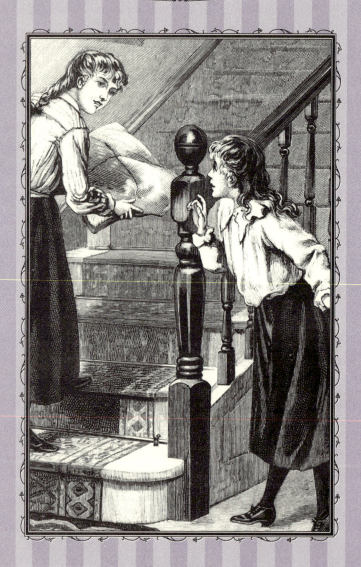

THE MAIL ON
CORRIDOR THREE

Winifred Kirkland

*R*uth Sutton carried the mail to all the rooms on Corridor Three. She was openly adored by every coed on the floor—even shy little Ursa Lake at the end of the hall. Then came an illness that proved to be a blessing to that shyest one.

But hovering above every student was a fear so real it could almost be tasted—the fear of yellow envelopes!

tout-booted, strong-shouldered Ruth Sutton went swinging down Corridor Three. Ruth could have distributed the mail much faster if so many doors had not flown open to welcome her three times each day. Her big hand had a ringing knock.

"More proof sheets, Miss Fletcher. Can't I come up and help you correct them tonight?"

No one else would have dared to offer help of any description to the austere Miss Fletcher.

"Proofs are bad for your headache," continued Ruth.

"Thank you, Ruth. Have you really time?"

On went Ruth.

"Carol Watkins, have you a mother who writes you once a day?"

"No, twice."

"And how often do you write her?"

"But, Ruth, I have so little time!"

"Make some, then!"

At the end of the corridor was a little room, perched at the top of a twisting staircase. Ruth always smiled at the big "Do Not Disturb" sign upon it, for who was likely to come seeking Ursa Lake? At first even Ruth had had to poke Ursa's mail under the closed door, but now it opened at the sound of her step on the stair, and a wistful little freshman hung over the balustrade.

"Nothing today, honey. I'm sorry. Perhaps he'll write tomorrow."

"Oh, it wasn't Father's letter I was looking for!" Ursa touched the empty mail sack. "You're sure there's not one at the very bottom for me—a yellow envelope?"

"Why, child, what do you know about yellow envelopes?"

"I hear the girls talk at the table. They say they come at the end of the first six weeks, then at the end of the first twelve, and last and worst at mid-year after examinations."

"They don't come at all to girls who study their heads off when they ought to be out playing tennis with their classmates. You ought to have more fun. I say, Ursa, I'll get Carol Watkins to take you over to the Open Fields today."

"Oh, please, please, Miss Sutton, don't!" cried Ursa, much perturbed. "She's a junior!"

"So am I a junior," answered Ruth.

Ursa's terrified shyness melted into a smile. "No, you're just you." Then she added: "You're sure I didn't get a flunk note—not in chemistry?"

"Not a sign of one. Why did you elect chemistry when you hate it so?"

"I had to! On account of Father."

"Did he want you to?"

Ursa flushed. "I never—I never can be sure that I know what Father wants. He—I—we—don't ever talk very much."

"I should think there was chemistry enough in your family already," said Ruth, laughing; "but of course the famous Professor Lake would want you to know his subject. That's the trouble with having a famous father."

Six weeks later there was again a trembling little Ursa for big Ruth to comfort.

"No, child, no yellow note this time either."

"I've worked so hard!"

"Hard enough to take a little time off now?" Ruth's arm went about Ursa's shoulders. "Miss Fletcher is in bed with one of her worst headaches. Can't you run down with me to my room and bring back my smelling salts?"

"And—and—take it—into her room—and give it to her!"

"Yes, Ursa. Don't you know anything about other people's headaches?"

"Yes, Father's. But I never dare to go to him. Ruth, it sometimes seems to me I'm afraid of everyone."

"College is a good place to get over that. People are really much nicer than chemistry."

"But you know why I work away at chemistry. Haven't you any parents yourself?"

It had never before occurred to Ursa to think about Ruth's home.

"One," Ruth answered briefly. Then, putting her hands on Ursa's shoulders, she said, "Tell me something. Have you ever been into *any* of the rooms on the corridor? Surely, some of the girls have come to see you?"

"All of them, the first week. I never went to see them. Why, Ruth, I couldn't! I don't know how to do it."

Carrying the mail after mid-year examinations is sometimes a sad task. During that week worry turned Ursa into a white-faced little wreck. Not until the last mail on Saturday was Ruth able to convince her that she had passed in all subjects, even in chemistry.

"All flunk notes have been sent out. I know, being mail carrier. It's time to write your father and tell him you're safe in everything. I'm glad about you, darling."

Ruth gave her a mighty hug.

"Ruth," said Ursa suddenly, "you are awfully good to me!"

What should there be in the touch of Ursa's hands that made big Ruth sink abruptly down on the window seat, flinging her mail bag to the floor? At first Ursa misunderstood.

"Ruth, you don't mean that there *is* a yellow note for me after all!"

Ruth lifted the mail pouch and shook a yellow envelope into her lap. "Not for you; not in chemistry. For me! In English!"

"Ruth, do you mean that you—"

"Have been afraid of a flunk note! Indeed, yes. Writing themes when I'm dead tired!"

"Oh Ruth,"—Ursa was on her knees by Ruth's side,—"it's perfectly terrible, isn't it?"

Ruth patted her hair.

"Well, it's not quite so serious as you look, darling! Never mind! But it is pretty hard, for it's worse for a junior to fail than for a freshman, and I don't see when I can find time to make up the failure. I don't see where I could squeeze in an extra minute."

"The mail takes a lot of time, doesn't it? Couldn't you give it up?"

"Give up fifteen dollars a month! No, little friend, I could not! I am working my way." Suddenly she leaned back and closed her eyes tight. "And back at home Mother is working my way, too. She isn't, you know, a famous chemist with plenty of money. She's just,"—Ruth's head went down into the pillows,—"she's just a darling little butter-and-eggs woman on a farm. My head—how it aches!"

Ursa had never before smoothed away a headache, but she did it that afternoon.

It was twilight when Ruth stirred on her bed and murmured, "What am I doing, taking on like this?"

"You're not taking on. I thought you were asleep. Ruth, won't your mother understand?"

Ruth's lips twitched grimly.

"There isn't much to understand. I've just failed, and I haven't time to study for another examination. That's all there is to understand."

A little voice was at Ruth's ear. "But you don't have to stop everywhere, to comfort everybody."

Ruth sat up. "I'm not sorry about that."

She looked so fierce that Ursa quavered, "I'm not sorry, either!"

Ruth sank back on the pillows. It was a new voice that roused her after a moment:

"I've only my allowance, and I'd never ask Father for more."

Ruth opened dancing eyes. "You child! Do you think I'd take anything from anyone?"

"Not from me? Why, I'd take anything from you! I'd do anything for you!"

"Ursa, there's only one thing I wanted you to do, and you haven't done that. You elected a course in chemistry for your father. I wish you'd elect a course in making friends for me."

But Ursa was still thinking of Ruth. "If somebody helped you, carrying the mail? If perhaps some other girl could carry it for you? And—and—give you the money?"

Ruth sat bolt upright. "Who?"

"Could I, Ruth? Do I know enough to sort letters?"

"It proves how little you know about me, or about people, that you should think I'd let you."

"But wouldn't it be a way for me to learn about people? I'd have to go into every one of those rooms downstairs. Miss Fletcher's. Miss Watson's,"—her cold little hands were clenched,—"three times a day! I couldn't do it for anyone except you."

A strange look came into Ruth's eyes. She looked into Ursa's uplifted face, and then out into the twilight. She was silent so long that the little freshman began to think that Ruth had been offended. Finally Ruth turned from the window.

"Perhaps, dear, as an experiment, I'll let you. Only—I couldn't let anyone do such a thing for me except you."

Corridor Three missed Ruth's swinging step and her booming voice. The new mail girl was frightened, furtive, but she was brave, and so Corridor Three encouraged her whispered "Good morning" until it grew more confident.

From her own door at the far end, Ruth could listen. She smiled one morning when a squeaky little voice tremulously asked at the door across the hall, "I hope your headache is better this morning, Miss Fletcher."

Meanwhile spring came again to the Open Fields, and they were gay with girls playing tennis; and then May went hurrying on, and there was the clatter of commencement preparations, and at last June came, and with it the examinations. In these days it was Ursa who brought the mail to Ruth's room—a tired little Ursa on that hot June afternoon.

"All the flunk notes are out, Ruth. You didn't get one. Your English is safe."

Ruth fell on Ursa with a hug. "Thanks be! And Mother need never know!"

But with a little cry Ursa opened a clenched fist on a crumpled yellow envelope. "But I did get a yellow note in chemistry! And Father will have to know, for my note says I must be tutored this summer." Her voice trembled, but she was trying to smile. "It—it—costs something, Ruth—a course in friendship. Father is coming to take me home when college closes on Saturday. I can't tell him."

"I will tell him," Ruth answered quietly.

On Saturday they went down to him together in the big reception hall. Ursa's father was tall, dark, distant. He turned politely questioning eyes toward the big girl who held Ursa's hand. He did not seem to know how to kiss Ursa, as the other arriving fathers kissed their daughters. Ursa mumbled a trembling introduction.

"Professor Lake," Ruth said at once. "I just came down for a moment with Ursa because we are friends, and because there is something to tell you, and Ursa thinks it's worse than it is—"

But here Ursa stood and looked straight up at her father.

"Father, I have failed in chemistry."

"In anything else?"

"She has honor marks in every other subject," said Ruth.

"Why did you elect chemistry, Ursa?" he demanded. "It's not your line."

"Because it's your line, Professor Lake," Ruth explained.

"But now that you've failed in it, you can drop the subject, Ursa?"

"Not until I've been tutored this summer!"

"Is that all? Well, perhaps I might manage to do that myself," he said with a smile.

"But, Father, have you time? For me?"

Ruth, watching them, wondered which was shyer, father or daughter.

"I shall have time," he said. "Afterward you can drop chemistry, I hope."

"Do you want me to?"

"I never wanted you to touch it."

"Why, but—"

"I sent you a thousand miles away from my laboratory, from me, Ursa, so that you might learn something—something more human than chemistry. That was my great hope. Instead," he shook his head wearily, "you elected to study chemistry."

"Oh," cried Ruth, "no! In the middle of the year she elected something else, and that's why she failed in chemistry. She carried the mail for me. I am working my way, and I needed—both time and money. Ursa made it possible for me to have both. I ought not to have let her, perhaps, but—"

"And did Ursa," he asked, "pass her course—in mail carrying?"

Ruth answered the longing hope in his eyes. "Yes. All the corridor loves her, but she doesn't know it." Ruth's hand slipped an instant into Ursa's, and then went out to Professor Lake's for one warm shake. "Good-by!" she said, and in a moment was gone from them, humming on her way.

"Ursa," said her father, "give up your chemistry. It is my line, but you," his deep eyes glowed, "are going to be different. I know chemistry, but I have never known how to win a friend like that."

Winifred Margaret Kirkland
(1872–1943)

of Columbia, Pennsylvania, besides writing many memorable short stories for inspirational journals early in the twentieth century, also wrote a number of books, including *Polly Pot's Parish, Christmas Bishop, Portrait of a Carpenter,* and *Star in the East.*

THE STRANGER WHO TAUGHT MAGIC

Arthur Gordon

Why is it that we listlessly move along through life—one day much like all the other days—and suddenly a spark will jump from a person we hardly know . . . and life is never the same again?

hat July morning, I remember, was like any other, calm and opalescent before the heat of the fierce Georgia sun. I was thirteen, sunburned, shaggy-haired, a little aloof, and solitary. In winter I had to put on shoes and go to school like everyone else. But summers I lived by the sea, and my mind was empty and wild and free.

On this particular morning, I had tied my rowboat to the pilings of an old dock upriver from our village. There, sometimes, the striped sheepshead lurked in the still, green water. I was crouched, motionless as a stone, when a voice spoke suddenly above my head: "Canst thou draw out leviathan with a hook? or his tongue with a cord which thou lettest down?"

I looked up, startled, into a lean pale face and a pair of the most remarkable eyes I had ever seen. It wasn't a question of color; I'm not sure, now, what color they were. It was a combination of things: warmth, humor, interest, alertness. *Intensity*—that's the word, I guess—and, underlying it all, a curious kind of mocking sadness. I believe I thought him old.

He saw how taken aback I was. "Sorry," he said. "It's a bit early in the morning for the Book of Job, isn't it?" He nodded at the two or three fish in the boat. "Think you could teach me how to catch those?"

Ordinarily, I was wary of strangers, but anyone interested in fishing was hardly a stranger. I nodded, and he climbed down into the boat. "Perhaps we should introduce ourselves," he said. "But then again, perhaps not. You're a boy willing to teach; I'm a teacher willing to learn. That's introduction enough. I'll call you *Boy,* and you call me *Sir.* "

Such talk sounded strange in my world of sun and salt water. But there was something so magnetic about the man, and so disarming about his smile, that I didn't care.

I gave him a hand line and showed him how to bait his hooks with fiddler crabs. He kept losing baits, because he could not recognize a sheepshead's stealthy tug, but he seemed content not to catch anything. He told me he had rented one of the weathered bungalows behind the dock. "I needed to hide for a while," he said. "Not from the police, or anything like that. Just from friends and relatives. So don't tell anyone you've found me, will you?"

I was tempted to ask where he was from; there was a crispness in the way he spoke that was very different from the soft accents I was accustomed to. But I didn't. He had said he was a teacher, though, and so I asked what he taught.

"In the school catalog they call it English," he said. "But I like to think of it as a course in magic—in the mystery and magic of words. Are you fond of words?"

I said that I had never thought much about them. I also pointed out that the tide was ebbing, that the current was too strong for more fishing, and that in any case it was time for breakfast.

"Of course," he said, pulling in his line. "I'm a little forgetful about such things these days." He eased himself back onto the dock with a little grimace, as if the effort cost him something. "Will you be back on the river later?"

I said that I would probably go casting for shrimp at low tide.

"Stop by," he said. "We'll talk about words for a while, and then perhaps you can show me how to catch shrimp."

So began a most unlikely friendship, because I did go back. To this day, I'm not sure why. Perhaps it was because, for the first time, I had met an adult on terms that were in balance. In the realm of words and ideas, he might be the teacher. But in my own small universe of winds and tides and sea creatures, the wisdom belonged to me.

Almost every day after that, we'd go wherever the sea gods or my whim decreed. Sometimes up the silver creeks, where the terrapin skittered down the banks and the great blue herons stood like statues. Sometimes along the ocean dunes, fringed with graceful sea oats, where by night the great sea turtles crawled and by day the wild goats browsed. I showed him where the mullet swirled and where the flounder lay in cunning camouflage. I learned that he was incapable of much exertion; even pulling up the anchor seemed to exhaust him. But he never complained. And, all the time, talk flowed from him like a river.

Much of it I have forgotten now, but some comes back as clear and distinct as if it all happened yesterday, not decades ago. We might be sitting in a hollow of the dunes, watching the sun go down in a smear of crimson. "Words," he'd say. "Just little black marks on paper. Just sounds in the empty air. But think of the power they have! They can make you laugh or cry, love or hate, fight or run away. They can heal or hurt. They even come to look and sound like what they mean. *Angry* looks angry on the page. *Ugly* sounds ugly when you say it. Here!" He would hand me a piece of shell. "Write a word that looks or sounds like what it means."

I would stare helplessly at the sand.

"Oh," he'd cry, "you're being dense. There are so many! Like *whisper . . . leaden . . . twilight . . . chime . . .* Tell you what: When you go to bed tonight, think of five words that look like what they mean and five that sound like what they mean. Don't go to sleep until you do!"

And I would try—but always fall asleep.

Or we might be anchored just offshore, casting into the surf for sea bass, our little bateau nosing over the rollers like a restless hound. "Rhythm," he would say. "Life is full of it; words should have it, too. But you have to train your ear. Listen to the waves on a quiet night; you'll pick up the cadence. Look at the patterns the wind makes in dry sand and you'll see how syllables in a sentence should fall. Do you know what I mean?"

My conscious self didn't know; but perhaps something deep inside me did. In any case, I listened.

I listened, too, when he read from the books he sometimes brought: Kipling, Conan Doyle, Tennyson's *Idylls of the King*. Often he would stop and repeat a phrase or a line that pleased him. One day, in Malory's *Le Morte d'Arthur*, he found one: "And the great horse grimly neighed." "Close your eyes," he said to me, "and say that slowly, out loud." I did. "How did it make you feel?" "It gives me the shivers," I said truthfully. He was delighted.

But the magic that he taught was not confined to words; he had a way of generating in me an excitement about things I had always taken for granted. He might point to a bank of clouds. "What do you see there? Colors? That's not enough. Look for towers and draw-bridges. Look for dragons and griffins and strange and wonderful beasts."

Or he might pick up an angry claw-brandishing blue crab, holding it cautiously by the back flippers as I had taught him. "Pretend you're this crab," he'd say. "What do you see through those stalklike eyes? What do you feel with those complicated legs? What goes on in your tiny brain? Try it for just five seconds. Stop being a boy. Be a crab!" And I would stare in amazement at the furious creature, feeling my comfortable identity lurch and sway under the impact of the idea.

So the days went by. Our excursions became less frequent, because he tired so easily. He brought two chairs down to the dock and some books, but he didn't read much. He seemed content to watch me as I fished, or the circling gulls, or the slow river coiling past.

A sudden shadow fell across my life when my parents told me I was going to camp for two weeks. On the dock that afternoon I asked my friend if he would be there when I got back. "I hope so," he said gently.

But he wasn't. I remember standing on the sun-warmed planking of the old dock, staring at the shuttered bungalow and feeling a hollow sense of finality and loss. I ran to Jackson's grocery store—where everyone knew everything—and asked where the schoolteacher had gone.

"He was sick, real sick," Mrs. Jackson replied. "Doc phoned his relatives up north to come get him. He left something for you—he figured you'd be asking for him."

She handed me a book. It was a slender volume of verse, *Flame and Shadow,* by someone I had never heard of: Sara Teasdale. The corner of one page was turned down, and there was a penciled star by one of the poems. I still have the book, with the poem "On the Dunes."

> *If there is any life when death is over,*
> *These tawny beaches will know much of me,*
> *I shall come back, as constant and as changeful*
> *As the unchanging, many-colored sea.*
> *If life was small, if it has made me scornful,*
> *Forgive me; I shall straighten like a flame*
> *In the great calm of death, and if you want me*
> *Stand on the sea-ward dunes and call my name.*

Well, I have never stood on the dunes and called his name. For one thing, I never knew it; for another, I'd be too self-conscious.

And there are long stretches when I forget all about him. But sometimes—when the music or the magic in a phrase makes my skin tingle, or when I pick up an angry blue crab, or when I see a dragon in the flaming sky—sometimes I remember.

Arthur Gordon
(born in 1912)

during his long and illustrious career, has edited such renowned journals as *Good Housekeeping, Cosmopolitan,* and *Guideposts.* Along the way, besides penning over two hundred of some of the finest short stories of our time, he also found time to write books such as *Reprisal, Norman Vincent Peale: Minister to Millions,* and *Red Carpet at the White House.* Today he and his wife, Pamela, still live on the Georgia coast he has loved since he was a child.

THE THIRD
INGREDIENT

O. Henry

*F*riends come in all shapes and sizes: Hands, Heads,
Muscles, Feet, Backs, Bosoms, and Shoulders. Hetty was
a Shoulder—had known it, and reluctantly come to terms
with it, a long time ago.

Down on her luck herself, that poor little fool down the
hall was down on her luck even more.

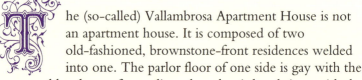he (so-called) Vallambrosa Apartment House is not an apartment house. It is composed of two old-fashioned, brownstone-front residences welded into one. The parlor floor of one side is gay with the wraps and headgear of a modiste; the other is lugubrious with the sophistical promises and grisly display of a painless dentist. You may have a room there for two dollars a week or you may have one for twenty dollars. Among the Vallambrosa's roomers are stenographers, musicians, brokers, shopgirls, space-rate writers, art students, wire-tappers, and other people who lean far over the banister-rail when the door-bell rings.

This treatise shall have to do with but two of the Vallambrosians— though meaning no disrespect to the others.

At six o'clock one afternoon Hetty Pepper came back to her third-floor rear $3.50 room in the Vallambrosa with her nose and chin more sharply pointed than usual. To be discharged from the department store where you have been working four years, and with only fifteen cents in your purse, does have a tendency to make your features appear more finely chiseled.

And now for Hetty's thumb-nail biography while she climbs the two flights of stairs.

She walked into the Biggest Store one morning four years before, with seventy-five other girls, applying for a job behind the waist department counter. The phalanx of wage-earners formed a bewildering scene of beauty, carrying a total mass of blond hair sufficient to have justified the horseback gallops of a hundred Lady Godivas.

The capable, cool-eyed, impersonal, young, bald-headed man whose task it was to engage six of the contestants was aware of a feeling of suffocation as if he were drowning in a sea of frangi-pani, while white clouds, hand-embroidered, floated about him.

And then a sail hove in sight. Hetty Pepper, homely of countenance, with small, contemptuous green eyes and chocolate-colored hair, dressed in a suit of plain burlap and a common-sense hat, stood before him with every one of her twenty-nine years of life unmistakably in sight.

"You're on!" shouted the bald-headed young man, and was saved. And that is how Hetty came to be employed in the Biggest Store. The story of her rise to an eight-dollar-a-week salary is the combined stories of Hercules, Joan of Arc, Una, Job, and Little Red Riding Hood. You shall not learn from me the salary that was paid her as a beginner. There is a sentiment growing about such things, and I want no millionaire store-proprietors climbing the fire escape of my tenement house to throw dynamite bombs into my skylight boudoir.

The story of Hetty's discharge from the Biggest Store is so nearly a repetition of her engagement as to be monotonous.

In each department of the store there is an omniscient, omnipresent, and omnivorous person carrying always a mileage book and a red necktie, and referred to as a "buyer." The destinies of the girls in his department who live on (see Bureau of Victual Statistics)—so much per week are in his hands.

This particular buyer was a capable, cool-eyed, impersonal, young, bald-headed man. As he walked along the aisles of his department he seemed to be sailing on a sea of frangipani, while white clouds, machine-embroidered, floated around him. Too many sweets bring surfeit. He looked upon Hetty Pepper's homely countenance, emerald eyes, and chocolate-colored hair as a welcome oasis of green in a desert of cloying beauty. In a quiet angle of a counter he pinched her arm kindly, three inches above the elbow. She slapped him three feet away with one good blow of her muscular and not especially lily-white right. So, now you know why Hetty Pepper came to leave the Biggest Store at thirty minutes' notice, with one dime and a nickel in her purse.

This morning's quotations list the price of rib beef at six cents per (butcher's) pound. But on the day that Hetty was "released" by the B. S., the price was seven and one half cents. That fact is what makes this story possible. Otherwise, the extra four cents would have—

But the plot of nearly all the good stories in the world is concerned with shorts who were unable to cover; so, you can find no fault with this one.

Hetty mounted with her rib beef to her $3.50 third-floor back. One hot, savory beef stew for supper, a night's good sleep, and she would be fit in the morning to apply again for the tasks of Hercules, Joan of Arc, Una, Job, and Little Red Riding Hood.

In her room she got the graniteware stew-pan out of the 2 x 4 foot china—er—I mean earthenware closet, and began to dig down in a rat's-nest of paper bags for the potatoes and onions. She came out with her nose and chin just a little sharper pointed.

There was neither a potato nor an onion. Now, what kind of a beef stew can you make out of simply beef? You can make oyster soup without oysters, turtle soup without turtles, coffee cake without coffee, but you can't make beef stew without potatoes and onions.

But rib beef alone, in an emergency, can make an ordinary pine door look like a wrought-iron, gambling-house portal to the wolf. With salt and pepper and a tablespoon of flour (first well stirred in a little cold water) 'twill serve—'tis not so deep as a lobster à la Newburgh, nor so wide as a church festival doughnut; but 'twill serve.

Hetty took her stew-pan to the rear of the third-floor hall. According to the advertisements of the Vallambrosa there was running water to be found there. Between you and me and the water-meter, it only ambled or walked through the faucets; but technicalities have no place here. There was also a sink where housekeeping roomers often met to dump their coffee grounds and glare at one another's kimonos.

At this sink Hetty found a girl with heavy, gold-brown, artistic hair and plaintive eyes washing two large "Irish" potatoes. Hetty knew the Vallambrosa as well as anyone not owning "double hextra-magnifying eyes" could compass its mysteries. The kimonos were her encyclopedia, her "Who's What?", her clearing-house of news, of goers and comers. From a rose-pink kimono edged with Nile green she had learned that the girl with the potatoes was a miniature-painter living in a kind of attic—or "studio," as they prefer to call it—on the top floor. Hetty was not certain in her mind what a miniature was; but it certainly wasn't a house; because house-painters, although they wear splashy overalls and poke ladders in your face on the street, are known to indulge in a riotous profusion of food at home.

The potato girl was quite slim and small, and handled her potatoes as an old bachelor uncle handles a baby who is cutting teeth. She had a dull shoemaker's knife in her right hand, and she had begun to peel one of the potatoes with it.

Hetty addressed her in the punctiliously formal tone of one who intends to be cheerfully familiar with you in the second round.

"Beg pardon," she said, "for butting into what's not my business, but if you peel them potatoes you lose out. They're new Bermudas. You want to scrape 'em. Lemme show you."

She took a potato and the knife, and began to demonstrate.

"Oh, thank you," breathed the artist. "I didn't know. And I *did* hate to see the thick peeling go; it seemed such a waste. But I thought they always had to be peeled. When you've got only potatoes to eat, the peelings count, you know."

"Say, kid," said Hetty, staying her knife, "you ain't up against it, too, are you?"

The miniature artist smiled starvedly.

"I suppose I am. Art—or, at least, the way I interpret it— doesn't seem to be much in demand. I have only these potatoes for my dinner. But they aren't so bad boiled and hot, with a little butter and salt."

"Child," said Hetty, letting a brief smile soften her rigid features, "Fate has sent me and you together. I've had it handed to me in the neck, too; but I've got a chunk of meat in my room as big as a lap-dog. And I've done everything to get potatoes except pray for 'em. Let's me and you bunch our commissary departments and make a stew of 'em. We'll cook it in my room. If we only had an onion to go in it! Say, kid, you haven't got a couple of pennies that've slipped down into the lining of your last winter's sealskin, have you? I could step down to the corner and get one at old Giuseppe's stand. A stew without an onion is worse'n a matinée without candy."

"You may call me Cecilia," said the artist. "No; I spent my last penny three days ago."

"Then we'll have to cut the onion out instead of slicing it in," said Hetty. "I'd ask the janitress for one, but I don't want 'em hep just yet to the fact that I'm pounding the asphalt for another job. But I wish we did have an onion."

In the shop-girl's room the two began to prepare their supper. Cecilia's part was to sit on the couch helplessly and beg to be allowed to do something, in the voice of a cooing ring-dove. Hetty prepared the rib beef, putting it in cold salted water in the stew-pan and setting it on the one-burner gas stove.

"I wish we had an onion," said Hetty, as she scraped the two potatoes.

On the wall opposite the couch was pinned a flaming, gorgeous advertising picture of one of the new ferry-boats of the P.U.F.F. Railroad that had been built to cut down the time between Los Angeles and New York City one eighth of a minute.

Hetty, turning her head during her continuous monologue, saw tears running from her guest's eyes as she gazed on the idealized presentment of the speeding, foam-girdled transport.

"Why, say, Cecilia, kid," said Hetty, poising her knife, "is it as bad art as that? I ain't a critic, but I thought it kind of brightened up the room. Of course, a manicure-painter could tell it was a bum picture in a minute. I'll take it down if you say so. I wish to the holy Saint Potluck we had an onion."

But the miniature miniature-painter had tumbled down, sobbing, with her nose indenting the hard-woven drapery of the couch. Something was here deeper than the artistic temperament offended at crude lithography.

Hetty knew. She had accepted her role long ago. How scant the words with which we try to describe a single quality of a human being! When we reach the abstract we are lost. The nearer to Nature that the babbling of our lips comes, the better do we understand. Figuratively (let us say), some people are Bosoms, some are Hands, some are Heads, some are Muscles, some are Feet, some are Backs for burdens.

Hetty was a Shoulder. Hers was a sharp, sinewy shoulder; but all her life people had laid their heads upon it, metaphorically or actually, and had left there all or half their troubles. Looking at Life anatomically, which is as good a way as any, she was preordained to be a Shoulder. There were few truer collarbones anywhere than hers.

Hetty was only thirty-three, and she had not yet outlived the little pang that visited her whenever the head of youth and beauty leaned upon her for consolation. But one glance in her mirror always served as an instantaneous painkiller. So she gave one pale look into the crinkly old looking-glass on the wall above the gas stove, turned down the flame a little lower from the bub-bling beef and potatoes, went over to the couch, and lifted Cecilia's head to its confessional.

"Go on and tell me, honey," she said. "I know now that it ain't art that's worrying you. You met him on a ferry-boat, didn't you? Go on, Cecilia, kid, and tell your—your Aunt Hetty about it."

But youth and melancholy must first spend the surplus of sighs and tears that waft and float the barque of romance to its harbor in the delectable isles. Presently, through the stringy tendons that formed the bars of the confessional, the penitent—or was it the glorified communicant of the sacred flame?—told her story with-out art or illumination.

"It was only three days ago. I was coming back on the ferry from Jersey City. Old Mr. Schrum, an art dealer, told me of a rich man in Newark who wanted a miniature of his daughter painted. I went to see him and showed him some of my work. When I told him the price would be fifty dollars he laughed at me like a hyena. He said an enlarged crayon twenty times the size would cost him only eight dollars.

"I had just enough money to buy my ferry ticket back to New York. I felt as if I didn't want to live another day. I must have looked as I felt, for I saw *him* on the row of seats opposite me, looking at me as if he understood. He was nice-looking, but, oh, above everything else, he looked kind. When one is tired or unhappy or hopeless, kindness counts more than anything else.

"When I got so miserable that I couldn't fight against it any longer, I got up and walked slowly out the rear door of the ferry-boat cabin. No one was there, and I slipped quickly over the rail, and dropped into the water. Oh, friend Hetty, it was cold, cold!

"For just one moment I wished I was back in the old Vallambrosa, starving and hoping. And then I got numb, and didn't care. And then I felt that somebody else was in the water close by me, holding me up. He had followed me, and jumped in to save me.

"Somebody threw a thing like a big, white doughnut at us, and he made me put my arms through the hole. Then the ferry-boat backed, and they pulled us on board. Oh, Hetty, I was so ashamed of my wickedness in trying to drown myself; and, besides, my hair had all tumbled down and was sopping wet, and I was such a sight.

"And then some men in blue clothes came around; and *he* gave them his card, and I heard him tell them he had seen me drop my purse on the edge of the boat outside the rail, and in leaning over to get it I had fallen overboard. And then I remembered having read in the papers that people who try to kill themselves are locked up in cells with people who try to kill other people, and I was afraid.

"But some ladies on the boat took me downstairs to the fur-nace-room and got me nearly dry and did up my hair. When the boat landed, *he* came and put me in a cab. He was all dripping himself, but laughed as if he thought it was all a joke. He begged me, but I wouldn't tell him my name nor where I lived, I was so ashamed."

"You were a fool, child," said Hetty, kindly. "Wait till I turn the light up a bit. I wish to Heaven we had an onion."

"Then he raised his hat," went on Cecilia, "and said: 'Very well. But I'll find you, anyhow. I'm going to claim my rights of salvage.' Then he gave money to the cab-driver and told him to take me where I wanted to go, and walked away. What is 'salvage,' Hetty?"

"The edge of a piece of goods that ain't hemmed," said the shop-girl. "You must have looked pretty well frazzled out to the little hero boy."

"It's been three days," moaned the miniature-painter, "and he hasn't found me yet."

"Extend the time," said Hetty. This is a big town. Think of how many girls he might have to see soaked in water with their hair down before he would recognize you. The stew's getting on fine—but, oh, for an onion! I'd even use a piece of garlic if I had it."

The beef and potatoes bubbled merrily, exhaling a mouth-watering savor that yet lacked something, leaving a hunger on the palate, a haunting, wistful desire for some lost and needful ingredient.

"I came near drowning in that awful river," said Cecilia, shuddering.

"It ought to have more water in it," said Hetty; "the stew, I mean. I'll go get some at the sink."

"It smells good," said the artist.

"That nasty old North River?" objected Hetty. "It smells to me like soap factories and wet setter-dogs—oh, you mean the stew. Well, I wish we had an onion for it. Did he look like he had money?"

"First he looked kind," said Cecilia. "I'm sure he was rich; but that matters so little. When he drew out his bill-fold to pay the cabman you couldn't help seeing hundreds and thousands of dollars in it. And I looked over the cab doors and saw him leave the ferry station in a motor-car; and the chauffeur gave him his bearskin to put on, for he was sopping wet. And it was only three days ago."

"What a fool!" said Hetty, shortly.

"Oh, the chauffeur wasn't wet," breathed Cecilia. "And he drove the car away very nicely."

"I mean *you*," said Hetty. "For not giving him your address."

"I never give my address to chauffeurs," said Cecilia, haughtily.

"I wish we had one," said Hetty, disconsolately.

"What for?"

"For the stew, of course—oh, I mean an onion."

Hetty took a pitcher and started to the sink at the end of the hall.

A young man came down the stairs from above just as she was opposite the lower step. He was decently dressed, but pale and haggard. His eyes were dull with the stress of some burden of physical or mental woe. In his hand he bore an onion—a pink, smooth, solid, shining onion, as large around as a ninety-eight-cent alarm clock.

Hetty stopped. So did the young man. There was something Joan of Arc-ish, Herculean and Una-ish in the look and pose of the shoplady—she had cast off the roles of Job and Little Red Riding Hood. The young man stopped at the foot of the stairs and coughed distractedly. He felt marooned, held up, attacked, assailed, levied upon, sacked, assessed, pan-handled, browbeaten, though he knew not why. It was the look in Hetty's eyes that did it. In them he saw the Jolly Roger fly to the masthead and an able seaman with a dirk between his teeth scurry up the ratlines and nail it there. But as yet he did not know that the cargo he carried was the thing that had caused him to be so nearly blown out of the water without even a parley.

"*Beg* your pardon," said Hetty, as sweetly as her dilute acetic-acid tones permitted, "but did you find that onion on the stairs? There was a hole in the paper bag; and I've just come out to look for it."

The young man coughed for half a minute. The interval may have given him the courage to defend his own property. Also, he clutched his pungent prize greedily, and, with a show of spirit, faced his grim waylayer.

"No," he said, huskily, "I didn't find it on the stairs. It was given to me by Jack Bevens, on the top floor. If you don't believe it, ask him. I'll wait until you do."

"I know about Bevens," said Hetty, sourly. "He writes books and things up there for the paper-and-rags man. We can hear the postman guy him all over the house when he brings them thick envelopes back. Say—do you live in the Vallambrosa?"

"I do not," said the young man. "I come to see Bevens sometimes. He's my friend. I live two blocks west."

"What are you going to do with the onion?—*begging* your pardon," said Hetty.

"I'm going to eat it."

"Raw!"

"Yes: as soon as I get home."

"Haven't you got anything else to eat with it?"

The young man considered briefly.

"No," he confessed; "there's not another scrap of anything in my diggin's to eat. I think old Jack is pretty hard up for grub in his shack, too. He hated to give up the onion, but I worried him into parting with it."

"Man," said Hetty, fixing him with her world-sapient eyes, and laying a bony but impressive finger on his sleeve, "you've known trouble, too, haven't you?"

"Lots," said the onion owner, promptly. "But this onion is my own property, honestly come by. If you will excuse me, I must be going."

"Listen," said Hetty, paling a little with anxiety. "Raw onion is a mighty poor diet. And so is a beef stew without one. Now, if you're Jack Bevens' friend, I guess you're all right. There's a little lady—a friend of mine—in my room there at the end of the hall. Both of us are out of luck; and we had just potatoes and meat between us. They're stewing now. But it ain't got any soul. There's something lacking to it. There's certain things in life that are naturally intended to fit and belong together. One is pink cheese-cloth and green roses, and one is ham and eggs, and one is Irish and trouble. And the other one is beef and potatoes *with* onions. And still another one is people who are up against it and other people in the same fix."

The young man went into a protracted paroxysm of coughing. With one hand he hugged his onion to his bosom.

"No doubt; no doubt," said he, at length. "But, as I said, I must be going because—"

Hetty clutched his sleeve firmly.

"Don't be ridiculous, Little Brother. Don't eat raw onions. Chip in toward the dinner and line yourself inside with the best stew you ever licked a spoon over. Must two ladies knock a young gentleman down and drag him inside for the honor of dining with 'em? No harm shall befall you, Little Brother. Loosen up and fall into line."

The young man's pale face relaxed into a grin.

"Believe I'll go with you," he said, brightening. "If my onion is as good as a credential, I'll accept the invitation gladly."

"It's as good as that, but better as seasoning," said Hetty. "You come and stand outside the door till I ask my lady friend if she has any objections. And don't run away with that letter of recommendation before I come out."

Hetty went into her room and closed the door. The young man waited outside.

"Cecilia, kid," said the shop-girl, oiling the sharp saw of her voice as well as she could, "there's an onion outside. With a young man attached. I've asked him in to dinner. You ain't going to kick, are you?"

"Oh, dear!" said Cecilia, sitting up and patting her artistic hair. She cast a mournful glance at the ferry-boat poster on the wall.

"Nit," said Hetty. "It ain't him. You're up against real life now. I believe you said your hero friend had money and automobiles. This is a poor skeesicks that's got nothing to eat but an onion. But he's easy-spoken and not a freshy. I imagine he's been a gentleman, he's so low down now. And we need the onion. Shall I bring him in? I'll guarantee his behavior."

"Hetty, dear," sighed Cecilia, "I'm so hungry. What difference does it make whether he's a prince or a burglar? I don't care. Bring him in if he's got anything to eat with him."

Hetty went back into the hall. The onion man was gone. Her heart missed a beat, and a gray look settled over her face except on her nose and cheek-bones. And then the tides of life flowed in again, for she saw him leaning out of the front window at the other end of the hall. She hurried there. He was shouting to someone below. The noise of the street overpowered the sound of her footsteps. She looked down over his shoulder, saw whom he was speaking to, and heard his words. He pulled himself in from the window-sill and saw her standing over him.

Hetty's eyes bored into him like two steel gimlets.

"Don't lie to me," she said, calmly. "What were you going to do with that onion?"

The young man suppressed a cough and faced her resolutely. His manner was that of one who had been bearded sufficiently.

"I was going to *eat* it," said he, with emphatic slowness, "just as I told you before."

"And you have nothing else to eat at home?"

"Not a thing."

"What kind of work do you do?"

"I am not working at anything just now."

"Then why," said Hetty, with her voice set on its sharpest edge, "do you lean out of a window and give orders to chauffeurs in green automobiles in the street below?"

The young man flushed, and his dull eyes began to sparkle.

"Because, madam," said he, in *accelerando* tones, "I pay the chauffeur's wages and I own the automobile—and also this onion—this onion, madam."

He flourished the onion within an inch of Hetty's nose. The shoplady did not retreat a hair's-breadth.

"Then why do you eat onions," she said, with biting contempt, "and nothing else?"

"I never said I did," retorted the young man, heatedly. "I said I had nothing to eat where I live. I am not a delicatessen storekeeper."

"Then why," pursued Hetty, inflexibly, "were you going to eat a raw onion?"

"My mother," said the young man, "always made me eat one for a cold. Pardon my referring to a physical infirmity; but you may have noticed that I have a very, very severe cold. I was going to eat the onion and go to bed. I wonder why I am standing here and apologizing to you for it?"

"How did you catch this cold?" went on Hetty, suspiciously.

The young man seemed to have arrived at some extreme height of feeling. There were two modes of descent open to him—a burst of rage or to surrender to the ridiculous. He chose wisely; and the empty hall echoed his hoarse laughter.

"You're a dandy," said he. "And I don't blame you for being careful. I don't mind telling you. I got wet. I was on a North River ferry a few days ago when a girl jumped overboard. Of course, I—"

Hetty extended her hand, interrupting his story.

"Give me the onion," she said.

The young man set his jaw a trifle harder.

"Give me the onion," she repeated.

He grinned, and laid it in her hand.

Then Hetty's infrequent, grim, melancholy smile showed itself. She took the young man's arm and pointed with her other hand to the door of her room.

"Little Brother," she said, "go in there. The little fool you fished out of the river is there waiting for you. Go on in. I'll give you three minutes before I come. Potatoes is in there, waiting. Go on in, Onions."

After he had tapped at the door and entered, Hetty began to peel and wash the onion at the sink. She gave a gray look at the gray roofs outside and the smile on her face vanished by little jerks and twitches.

"But it's us," she said, grimly, to herself, "it's *us* that furnished the beef."

William Sidney Porter
(1862–1910)

was his name, but the world knows him simply as O. Henry, author of "The Gift of the Magi." Like the famous caliph of Baghdad who roamed city streets incognito looking for stories, just so did O. Henry, in his magical "Baghdad by the Hudson"— New York—with its 4 million stories to tell.

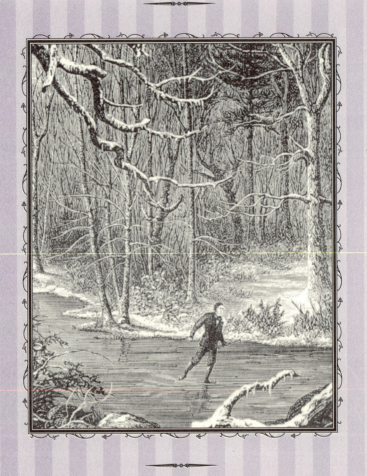

FIRST HONORS

Richard Marden

Two young men—one rich, one poor. One studied just enough to avoid dismissal; the other studied every moment not taken by work, for he had no one to pay his way.

First honors were in sight for Dave—then his friend Bob foolishly showed off on ice. When he fell through the ice, that act changed everything!

t seemed as if the entire population under twenty years of age had turned out to give Bob Scott and Dave Wood a big send-off as they started for college.

"I say, Bob, write to a fellow sometimes, won't you?" drawled Alec Towers, a tall, lazy-looking but by no means lazy-acting lad, arrayed in the latest style of sweater and knickers.

Bob nodded.

As the train was just moving out of the gray stone, ivy-hung station, a girl ran from the crowd, while a shout of laughter followed her.

"For you, David," she said, thrusting into his hand a small package. "It isn't anything, only a calendar—to mark the days."

Dave took the square package, waved his cap, smiled in his cheerful way that smile which had made him a favorite at Horner High, and the train whistled loudly as it rushed through the valley, leaving the town and the merry crowd of young folks behind.

"Well, we're off," grinned Bob, throwing himself back on the seat. "Off for college, old chap. I say, you might have let me pay the difference between this coach and the chair car. We'd have been lots more comfortable."

David flushed a little, the color sweeping up over his blond skin till it reached the wave of fair hair which he tried in vain every morning to brush flat.

"You know that I couldn't let you, Bob. We'd better begin as we're to go on. I have very little money, and must earn my way. Don't mind me a bit. You take a chair and have all the good things you can; it won't bother me."

Bob slapped his friend on the knee and laughed.

"You're telling the truth, boy. It will not bother you. You've never minded at all that I could do what I wanted to, as far as money is concerned, just because my father happened to strike it rich and yours didn't. I never saw a fellow like you. Dave, honest truth, I'd rather be in this stuffy coach with you than in a chair all by myself. There's just one thing sure, though; it's on me to pay for dinner in the dining car."

"Can't get ahead of me there, either," responded Dave. "Louise put up a big lunch—sandwiches, cake, and I don't know what else. It's good, all right, for Louise can cook, and she said there'd be plenty for you."

"Beaten all around," groaned Bob. "I give in gladly, knowing what kind of sandwiches Louise can make. What was that Loa gave you just as we pulled out?"

"Nothing but a calendar," he said.

"Mighty brave of Loa Bliss to go into that decorating shop after her father died and there wasn't anything left. Fine girl, Loa."

Dave did not answer. He, too, thought that Loa Bliss was a fine girl. It had been such a happy group of boys and girls: Loa and Louise, Bob Scott and Alec Towers. Funny that the circle should have broken so suddenly. Loa had gone to work as soon as she graduated from high school. She and her mother had sold their lovely home, and lived in two rooms with a tiny kitchenette; but the debts were all paid. Louise had her hands full keeping house for Mr. Wood, who had never been strong, and was what some people—Levi Scott, prosperous mill owner, among them—call a failure. Louise and David did not regard him in that way; they knew against what odds their father had fought.

Now, at last, Dave's dream was to be realized: he was actually going to college, and it had come about through his own efforts. A prize of one hundred dollars had been offered by Levi Scott for the best essay on the labor question. David won it, and his father said he was to do what he liked with it. He had liked to go with Bob to college. Beyond this small sum, Dave had nothing; but he was not afraid to work or ashamed to do anything that was honest. So he fixed his eyes upon the stars and blithely, cheerily went on his chosen way.

On his bureau in the small room which he found in the house of Miss Marla Smith, for which he paid by tending to her furnace, he placed the calendar which Loa had given him. Day by day he crossed off the dates. At Christmas time he could not go home for the simple reason that he had not enough money. "Good-bye" he waved to Bob, that blithe youth who had found more time for diversion than for study during that first semester, as he mounted the platform of the home-going train.

Trudging back to Miss Marla Smith's house, Dave had a queer, lonesome feeling. Never before had he been away from Father and Louise at Christmas time. The air was raw and cold. Miss Smith, wrapped in an old gray shawl and with cotton in her ears, remarked that she thought it felt like snow, and would David please cut a lot of wood, "so's to hev it handy if there come a cold snap."

The exercise did Dave good. He tossed off his cap, pulled back that wavy lock of hair which was such a nuisance, and went at the job with a will. What was that megaphone message which Bob had sent back on the breeze? Sounded like "look out for surprises," but maybe he had misunderstood it.

Dave began to whistle, piled his wood neatly, and came in to find Miss Smith dishing up stew and dumplings.

"Better set down an' eat something," she urged. "I've been thinkin' that while the vacation's on, you'd better eat your meals here. I'm kind of lonesome, anyway."

"It's–it's–very good of you, Miss Smith," stammered Dave.

"Oh, I dunno about that. Somehow it seems as if at Christmas time folks ought to sort of get together. That friend of yours is kind of shif'less, ain't he?"

"Who, Bob Scott? Oh, no, Miss Smith, he isn't shiftless."

Miss Smith sniffed.

"Seems to spend his time ridin' around in that big red car o' his. Ain't much time for a studyin', I reckon."

Dave laughed.

"Well, he isn't very strong on that line, but he doesn't need to be. His father is a very rich man."

"All the more reason why he should have somethin' in his brains," replied Miss Smith, with her nose in the air. "Reckon you kin beat him all holler."

"Maybe I could," answered Dave, speaking out his thought, "but it takes so much time to do the work necessary to earn my way, that I'm too tired at night to study as I should."

If Dave had looked up, he would have seen a very kind expression in Miss Smith's eyes.

"I made a nice custard pie." She added to herself, *I don't believe he's had enough to eat. I'll fix that all right.*

It was on the day after Christmas that the "surprise" really came. It had snowed hard, but automobiles were now running. When a huge limousine rolled up to Miss Smith's door, that lady did not appear in the least startled. Instead, dressed in her best black silk, wearing the brooch containing her father's miniature, with some little curls in her gray hair, she welcomed what seemed to be an avalanche of young people.

There were Louise, Alec Towers (as usual immaculately arrayed), Bob Scott, chuckling over the success of his surprise—and Loa, her cheeks glowing from the frosty air, her dark eyes shining with excitement and the delight of seeing Dave again.

And what a dinner Miss Smith had prepared for them! They had to squeeze into the tiny dining room, and there were no stately waiters such as Bob and Alec were accustomed to; but what did that matter? The boys insisted on waiting at tables, and wiped the dishes for the girls afterward. Miss Smith laughed at their jokes till she had to wipe away the tears.

Alec Towers had brought them over. He put on his costly fur coat, drew on his heavy gloves, and called to the crowd to hurry up; it would be dark before they got back to Horner, and it was beginning to snow.

"I brought another calendar for you, Dave," said Loa.

"I'm glad; I've marked off the days. At spring vacation I'm going home, if I have to walk."

"He can ride over with us now," put in Alec. "Funny I didn't think of it before. Come on, Dave, get your coat."

Miss Smith was watching Dave with a peculiar expression on her grim face.

For a moment Dave hesitated. Of course, there was plenty of room—he could go as well as not. Why shouldn't he?

"Sorry," he answered. "Good of you to ask me, Alec, but who'd attend to Miss Smith's furnace? She's lame and can't go up and down the cellar stairs of this house carrying coal. . . . Good-bye all!"

When the exuberant crowd was gone, the house was very still. Dave tried not to think about the fun they would have riding over to Horner, and Bob was to give a New Year's party—oh well!

"David," said plain Miss Smith, "I'll need a lot of help during the spring, cleaning up the garden and other things. I just want you to keep right on eatin' here. It's company for me, an' it won't hurt you to live on my vittles."

ne by one the years passed, Bob going gleefully, cheerfully, through his course, beloved of his professors, making no great splurge in his studies, but pulling through, to the satisfaction—and, it must be confessed, the surprise—of Levi Scott, financier.

"At any rate, you'll pull through, I reckon," his father remarked, as the two occupied easy chairs on the front porch of his comfortable home on a hot September evening.

"Guess I will," replied Bob, in his careless way. Then, speaking more seriously than was usual with him, "I wish that I had the courage and patience that Dave has shown."

"What about him?"

"He has lived with that not-in-the-least-attractive Miss Smith, tended her furnace, planted her garden, done all sorts of odd jobs, and kept up his studies, too. Honestly, Father, I don't see how he's done it. And he's not a mere 'grind,' either. There isn't a better runner in college, and as for swimming—the rest of us simply are not in it."

"What's he goin' to do when he gets through next year?" asked Bob's father, in an indifferent way.

"I don't know. He wants to go into business. You'd better give him my job, Dad," Bob laughed. "I've half a mind to make something of myself after all. Hello! There's Louise, going over to Loa's. Guess I'll walk along with her. Dave'll be sure to be there."

Loa *was* popular. The porch was always crowded in vacation time. She worked all day, but in the evening, dressed in soft white, her dark hair smooth and shining, her dark eyes sparkling with the joy of life, Loa dispensed lemonade to an admiring group.

Dave was there, sure enough, and so was Alec Towers, with half a dozen others, all talking at once.

Bob and Louise joined the group, Bob unusually quiet.

"What's the matter with you, Robert Scott?" demanded Alec. "Why not act festive if you don't feel so?"

"I'm thinking," answered Bob, solemnly.

"Thinking! Ladies and gentlemen, a miracle has happened. Bob thinks! Let silence reign."

There was dead stillness. Somebody stopped the phonograph in the midst of an operatic shriek. Only the clink of ice in tall glasses and the call of a katydid, prophesying frost, was heard. Then everybody laughed, and Bob became, as usual, the center of merriment.

He remained after the others left, sitting on the steps in the moonlight, at Loa's slippered feet. Again he was silent. Loa, being a sensible girl, knew how to be quiet also.

"Dave's doing fine at college," he said. "Shouldn't be surprised if he takes first honors."

"That's nice," replied Loa, rocking calmly, and wondering why Bob Scott seemed pale.

"I-I don't like to butt in, Loa, it isn't my way. Only I've got to say this, even if you don't like it. Dave's my friend; he's working awfully hard, and won't accept any lift on the journey through college. But he's—he's worth ten of a fellow who has the highest-priced automobile and rolls in money, an' don't you forget it, Loa. You know what fellow I mean."

Yes, Loa knew very well. Bob meant Alec Towers. He thought that she, a girl who was earning her living, was longing for the luxury which Alec Towers could give her. She smiled to herself. Bob didn't really know her.

So Dave was working for first honors, was he? Just like David. Loa smiled again as she closed the door and shut the moonlight out.

On a February afternoon just before the midyear examinations, the lake was black with moving figures of students at the college, both men and women. Bob was a crack skater and—a weakness he had—was fond of showing off, of cutting initials on the clear greenish, blue ice, of twirling and dancing on one foot. In order to have a free field for his exhibition, he took possession of a part of the lake from which the fellows had been warned away by a guard, who had, unfortunately, left his post for a moment.

"Don't skate there, Bob," Dave called out, sharply.

It was too late. With a sharp crack the ice, loosened by a recent thaw, gave way, and Bob sank into the black water.

Nobody realized the danger until Bob went under the ice. It was all over so quickly.

The crowd of gazers stood paralyzed. Then a figure, casting off his red sweater, broke through the line and plunged in after Bob. In a few seconds, his head emerged. With a mighty effort, he lifted out the inert body of Robert Scott, but in doing so, another large point of ice broke off, and while Bob was drawn safely to shelter, Dave was lost to sight.

By this time, the guard had returned, took in the situation, brought long planks, and with the assistance of some athletic students, succeeded in bringing Dave to the surface, unconscious but alive.

In the weeks which followed, before David Wood could get back to work, Bob haunted the infirmary. Faithfully, he brought news of the progress of the class, but Dave was too weak to care whether he ever studied again. His father came, and Louise. Soon the room became a lively center, full of beautiful spring flowers, music, and laughter. Before the month of April had passed, Dave was back at Miss Smith's, ready for work but well aware that his chance for first honors was gone. Never mind, he'd do his best.

Bob wrote to his father. "Dave saved my life. And now he'll miss his *summa cum laude.*"

The next morning he received a night letter from his busy father, who preferred this mode of correspondence.

"Never mind first honors. I'd take that boy if he was at the foot of his class. You tell him that the day after he graduates there's a good job waiting for him in Levi Scott's employ. God bless him!"

Commencement day came, a glorious morning, gold and green and decorated with roses. Louise was in the audience, and beside her was Loa. Dave had already shown her that he had marked off the last college day on the eighth semester calendar she had given him.

The President announced the list of honors, but David's name was not there.

Somebody from the gallery shouted, "Dave Wood! Where's Dave?"

Instantly the whole student body was on its feet. The audience rose, not knowing what it was all about, but wanting to share in the fun. Cheer followed cheer, handkerchiefs waved, the scent of roses and lilies was in the air.

"Come up here, Wood," said the President gravely.

Black-haired Levi Scott clapped until his face grew scarlet. Miss Smith's hat got crooked on her head, when the President—grave, solemn "Prexy"—shook hands with Dave, and smiled.

"I congratulate you, Wood," he said.

Dazed, almost frightened at this unexpected demonstration, Dave stumbled back to his seat. But as he did so, he looked at Loa. Her dark eyes were glowing with that beautiful light which he had hoped to see there if he won first honors.

He had not "lost his chance." The best chance of all was yet to come.

THE TAIL OF
THE LOBO

Penny Porter

*We are conditioned to fear the very word: wolf! Images of savage snarling, snapping, ravenous predators closing in for the kill swiftly come to mind whenever we think of the species. Consequently, to imagine that a wolf could possibly become a friend—*Dances with Wolves *notwithstanding—seems preposterous. And so it was that when a mother saw her three-year-old daughter leaning over to pet a great wolf, her heart froze with fear.*

 had just finished washing the lunch dishes when the screen door slammed and Becky, my three-year-old, rushed in. "Mommy!" she cried. "Come see my new doggy! I gave him water two times already. He's so thirsty!"

I sighed. Another of Becky's imaginary dogs. After our old dog died, our remote home—Singing Valley Ranch in Sonoita, Arizona—had become a lonely place for Becky. We planned to buy a puppy, but in the meantime "pretend" puppies popped up everywhere.

"Please come, Mommy," Becky said, her brown eyes enormous. "He's crying, and he can't walk."

Now, that *was* a twist. All her previous make-believe dogs could do marvelous tricks. Why suddenly a dog that couldn't walk?

"All right, honey," I said. But Becky had disappeared into the mesquite by the time I followed.

"Over here by the oak stump. Hurry, Mommy!" she called. I parted the thorny branches and raised my hand to shade my eyes from the desert sun. A numbing chill gripped me.

There she was, sitting on her heels, and cradled in her lap was the unmistakable head of a wolf. Beyond the head rose massive black shoulders. The rest of the body lay completely hidden inside the hollow stump of a fallen oak.

"Becky!" My mouth felt dry. "Don't move." I stepped closer. Pale yellow eyes narrowed. Black lips tightened, exposing double sets of two-inch fangs. Suddenly the wolf trembled; a piteous whine rose from his throat.

"It's awright, boy," crooned Becky. "Don't be afraid. That's my mommy, and she loves you, too."

Then the unbelievable happened. As her tiny hands stroked the great shaggy head, I heard the gentle *thump, thump, thumping* of the wolf's tail from deep inside the stump.

What was wrong with the animal? Why couldn't he get up? Of course! Could it be rabies? Hadn't Becky said, "He's so thirsty"? My memory flashed back to the five skunks who last week had torn the burlap from a leaking pipe in a frenzied effort to reach water during the final agonies of rabies.

I had to get Becky away. "Honey." My throat tightened. "Put-his-head-down-and-come-to-Mommy. We'll go find help."

Becky got up, kissed the wolf on the nose, and walked slowly to my outstretched arms. Sad yellow eyes followed her. Then the wolf's head sank to the ground.

With Becky safe in my arms, I ran to my car parked by the house and sped to the barns where Jake, one of the cowhands, was saddling up. "Jake. Come quickly. Becky found a wolf in the oak stump near the wash. I think it has rabies."

Back at the house I put my tearful child down for her nap. "But I want to give my doggy his water," she cried.

I kissed her and gave her some stuffed animals to play with. "Let Mommy and Jake take care of him for now," I said.

Moments later I reached the oak stump. "It's a Mexican lobo, all right," he said, "and a big one!"

The wolf whined, and then we both caught the smell of gangrene.

"Whew! It's not rabies," Jake said. "But he's sure hurt bad. Shall I put him out of his misery?"

The word *yes* was on my lips, but never spoken. Becky emerged from the bushes. "Is Jake going to make him well, Mommy?" She hauled the beast's head into her lap once more.

She buried her face in the coarse, dark fur. This time I wasn't the only one who heard the thumping echo of the lobo's tail.

That afternoon my husband, Bill, and our veterinarian came to see the wolf. Observing the trust the animal had in our child, Doc said to me, "Suppose you let Becky and me tend to this fella together." Minutes later, as child and vet reassured the stricken beast, the hypodermic found its mark. The yellow eyes closed.

"He's asleep now," said the vet. "Give me a hand here, Bill." They pulled the massive body out of the stump. The animal must have been five and a half feet long, and well over one hundred pounds. The hip and leg had been mutilated by bullets. Doc peeled away the rotten flesh. He dug out bone splinters, cleaned the wound, and gave the wolf a dose of penicillin. Next day he returned and inserted a metal rod, replacing the missing bone.

"Well, it looks like you've got yourselves a Mexican lobo," Doc said. "They don't tame real easy. I'm amazed at the way this fella took to your little gal."

Becky named the wolf Ralph, and carried food and water to the stump every day. Ralph's recovery was not easy. For three months he dragged his injured hindquarters by clawing the earth with his front paws. From the way he lowered his eyelids when we massaged the atrophied limbs, we knew he endured excruciating pain, but not once did he ever try to bite the hands of those who cared for him.

Four months to the day later, Ralph finally stood unaided. His huge frame shook as long-unused muscles were activated. Bill and I patted and praised him. But it was Becky to whom he turned for a gentle word, a kiss, or a smile. He responded to these gestures of love by swinging his great bushy tail like a pendulum.

As his strength grew, Ralph followed Becky all over the ranch. Together they roamed the desert pastures, the golden-haired child often stooping low, sharing with the great lame wolf whispered secrets of nature's wonders. When evening came, he would return like a silent shadow to his hollow stump.

As he wandered the ranch, Ralph never chased the cattle. However, his excessive drooling when I let my chickens run loose prompted my husband to build a fenced-in poultry yard.

And what a watchdog he was! Feral dogs and coyotes became only memories at Singing Valley Ranch. Ralph was king.

Becky's first day of school was sad for Ralph. When the bus left, he refused to return to the yard. Instead, he lay by the side of the road and waited. When Becky returned, he limped and tottered in wild, joyous circles around her. This welcoming ritual remained unchanged throughout her school years.

Although Ralph seemed happy on the ranch, he disappeared into the Santa Catalina Mountains for several weeks during the spring mating season, leaving us to worry about his safety. This was calving season, and fellow ranchers watched for the coyote, the cougar and, of course, the lone wolf. But Ralph was lucky.

Year after year we wondered about his mate and the pups he undoubtedly sired. We learned that the wolf returns to his mate to help feed the young. We wondered how much of Ralph's own food he dragged off to his hidden family. Each June, Becky gave him extra food because he grew so thin.

During Ralph's twelve years on our ranch, the habits of his life became rituals, and his love for our child never wavered. At last the spring came when he returned home with another bullet wound. The day after Ralph's injury, some ranchers whose land bordered ours told us they'd got a big she-wolf. The mate had been shot at also, but he kept running.

Becky was fifteen years old now. She sat with Ralph's head resting on her lap. He, too, must have been about fifteen and was gray with age. As Bill removed the bullet, my memory spun back through the years. Once again I saw a chubby three-year-old stroking the head of a huge black wolf.

The wound wasn't serious, but Ralph didn't get well. Precious pounds fell away, and his trips to the yard in search of Becky's loving companionship ceased. All day long he rested quietly.

But when night fell, old and stiff as he was, he disappeared into the hills. And each morning his food was gone.

The day came when we found him dead in front of the oak stump. The yellow eyes were closed. A lump in my throat choked me as I watched Becky stroke his shaggy neck, tears streaming down her face. "I'll miss him so," she cried.

As I covered him with a blanket, we were startled by a strange rustling sound from inside the stump. Becky looked inside. Two tiny yellow eyes peered back, and puppy fangs glinted in the semi-darkness. Ralph's pup. The motherless pup he had tried to care for alone.

Had a dying instinct told Ralph his offspring would be safe here, as he had been, with those who loved him? Hot tears spilled on baby fur as Becky gathered the trembling bundle in her arms.

"It's all right . . . little . . . Ralphie," she murmured. "Don't be afraid. That's my mom, and she loves you, too."

Did I hear a distant echo then? A gentle *thump, thump, thump-ing*—the tail of the lobo?

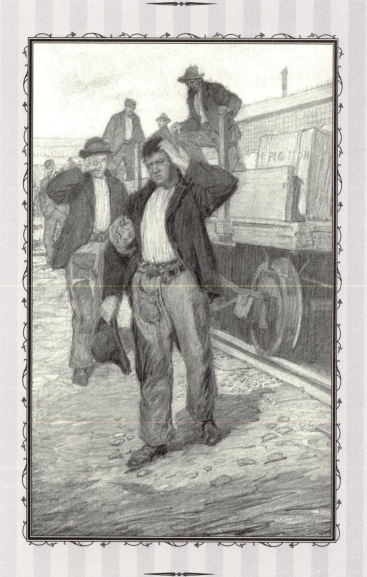

THE REBIRTH
OF TONY

Sherman Rogers

Today, he determined, that swearing ol' grouch Tony would be fired! But before he could implement his decision, the Scottish owner of the logging camp said something that gave him pause. He watched, and then he spoke.

Neither life was ever the same again. In the process, both learned a great deal about this elusive thing called "friendship" and what a difference a few kind words can make.

e have a big towheaded son by the name of Tony. Many people have asked me, "Why the name?"

Well, forty-three years ago I worked in an Idaho logging camp. We cut and trimmed the logs in the summer and skidded them four miles to the river on sleds after the fall snows. Along the route were three steep hills. I sanded hill number one. A belligerent Italian named Tony handled hill number two, the most dangerous.

Tony's life was one long grouch. He could speak little of the King's English but could swear in practically every language under the sun, and did. I had never heard anyone say a friendly word to him, and it was only natural that he never made any kind remarks in reply.

One morning the camp superintendent told me that he was going to town and would leave me in charge of the road crew. Being only twenty years old, I was considerably puffed up. However, with some misgivings, I asked what to do if the men didn't follow orders.

"Fire them," the superintendent snapped.

"Good," I answered. "You get another road crew because you'll meet these fellows coming out before you get back."

Shortly after he left, the old Scotsman who owned the camp appeared. "Now, look here," he said, "you're the foreman now and I will not interfere with your authority. But I know you intend to fire Tony."

"You must be a mind reader," I said.

"Well," he observed, "I would feel very bad about that. I've been logging forty years, and Tony is the most reliable man I ever had. I know he's a grouch, and I know he hates everything around him, but the fact remains that he is on the job before anyone else and he never quits until everyone else has gone. And there hasn't been an accident on that hill since he came eight years ago. There were men or horses killed there every year before he came. But go ahead and use your own judgment."

The moment he was out of sight, I started off to tell Tony something I'd been itching to tell him. Coming in sight of hill number two, I stood looking at him for several minutes before I realized what he was doing.

Road sanding is a peculiar job. As the teamster approaches, the sander walks ahead and drops just the right amount of sand into the ice-filled ruts to keep the heavy sled in slow motion. But that wasn't what Tony was doing at this particular moment.

The weather then stood about zero. Tony was drying a shovelful of sand over a small fire. He had no heavy clothes but was dressed in overalls. Instead of warming his lightly clad body, he was drying sand to make it easier and safer for the teamster; this was an extra precaution not in the rule book.

I walked over to Tony and said, "Good morning. Do you know I'm boss today?" Tony just grunted.

"Well," I went on, "do you know that I had every intention of firing you?" Another understanding grunt.

"But," I added, "no one's going to fire you." Tony looked up.

Then I told him, word for word, what the Scotsman had said to me.

Tony dropped the shovelful of sand he was holding. Tears were dropping down his face. "Why he no tell me dat eight years 'go?" he asked.

I made myself scarce right quick and did not see Tony anymore that day. That night when the teamsters came in to wash up, the lead teamster yelled excitedly, "Have you fellows seen the Wop? He's thrown enough sand today to sand a dozen hills; he's flown up and down as if he had wings. That guy actually smiled all day!"

That night as it was getting dark I heard a shout, "Hey, Boss!" It was Tony. He asked me if I would come home to supper with him.

I said, "Can you cook?"

"No," he answered, "I'm no cook. Marie—she cook."

"You don't mean to tell me you're married?" I blurted out.

"Sure ting," he said, and added shyly, "we gotta four keeds—da finest afour keeds."

We walked fast, for the thermometer still was about zero. Finally we came to a small clearing in which was a log house.

Tony put his fingers to his lips and blew a blast, and instantly the door flew open. Out tumbled a woman as broad as she was tall, and back of her came four small children. Tony yelled excitedly as he ran to gather them in his arms.

Here was a man I had always thought of as an ill-tempered grouch but who actually was a kind and loving father. "Come on in, Boss!" Tony yelled. "Da sup' she's a re'd."

During the meal Tony and Marie carried on a continuous flow of excited talk in Italian. Suddenly Marie jumped up and kissed me.

"Hey," I said, "what's this?"

"I justa tol' Marie you first foreman in deesa country who ever say, 'Good work, Tony,' an' it make Marie feel like Christmas."

Well, I could tell a long story about that night. I saw a woman kneel beside her children's bed and pray in broken English for them to grow up to be good American children. And she asked her Maker if He wouldn't please try to make American children understand her children, and not call them "Wops."

Later she told me how her two sons came home from school

and told her about the gibes they received because their clothes were poor and their speech imperfect. I began to understand how much suffering is caused by the contemptuous remarks that youngsters of foreign parentage have to endure.

A couple of days later I went to the schoolhouse, had the two Italian children excused, and then made a plea to the boys and girls to give these two youngsters a chance. I left the camp shortly after, but not before I learned that that was the end of the remarks and the beginning of happier days for the children.

Twelve years later I was walking down a logging railroad in Washington's rugged Olympic Peninsula, looking for a friend's camp. Suddenly I saw a man on top of the grade. He stood straight as a gun barrel and was neatly dressed. I yelled at him, asked directions to the camp, and waited for a reply. He just stared at me, and I yelled again, and then he started running to me. Then I recognized him.

"Tony!" I yelled. "What on earth are you doing here?"

Tony grinned back. "I'm da bigga push here."

Tony had become superintendent of railroad construction in one of the largest logging outfits in the West. He told me about his family. They were all fine, and the older son was going to the University of Washington. And then Tony said, "If it no be for da one minute you talka to me back in Idaho, I keel somebody someday. One minute—she change my whole life. You spend hour down in schoolroom—and she change lives my keeds, too." And he said, "I wonder why more people don't try understan' more an' hate less."

And I said to Tony, "I've been wondering about that for twelve years."

A WOMAN TO WARM
YOUR HEART BY

Dorothy Walworth

In each of our lives, if we are fortunate, we will rub shoulders with a real teacher. Not just a teacher who knows content or skills, not just a teacher who is interesting and projects well, not just a teacher who has a good sense of humor and a pleasing personality, and not just a teacher who rings true or has unquestioned integrity.

No, as special as all these traits are, there is a magical ingredient that can represent a life-or-death difference: Does that teacher truly care about each student as a friend, really empathize? Is that teacher willing to go all out to challenge each student to reach for the stars?

Miss Hungerford was just such a teacher.

n Cornwall, an old Hudson River town at the foot of Storm King Mountain, a story began fifty years ago and has not yet ended. When I visited there last winter, the older people of the town told me about it. It is a story they are proud to remember. "She is a woman to warm your heart by," they told me. "And as for him . . ."

That September, when it all started, Cornwall's seventy eighth grade and high school pupils sat in a schoolroom only big enough for twenty, waiting for a new teacher from upstate—an old maid in her thirties named Frances Irene Hungerford.

One of the high school students was Steve Pigott, a tall, lanky seventeen-year-old. Steve was good at his studies, but his father didn't see what use school was. He kept telling Steve, "You're old enough to cut out that foolishness." Pat Pigott was an Irish immigrant farmer who couldn't read or write.

Everyone was nice to Steve, but there was a difference, and he knew it. This was his second year in high school and he figured it would be his last. When the other boys talked about how they were going to make something of themselves, Steve never said a word.

Miss Hungerford turned out to be so small that when Steve stretched out his arm she could stand under it. But she stood straight as a footrule; she had steady deep-blue eyes, and when you looked into them you knew that all the winds over Storm King wouldn't budge her an inch. Her voice was pitched low, and her smile was like turning up a lamp.

One of the first things Miss Hungerford did was to write a sentence on the blackboard: "Seest thou the man who is diligent in his business? He shall stand before Kings." The schoolroom smothered giggles over that—as if anybody in Cornwall was ever going to get anywhere near a king!

In a week she had the high school wrapped around her little finger. If some of the boys had deviltry up their sleeves, she'd just smile, and her smile took the tuck right out of them. Every morning, at assembly, the eighth grade and high school sang. Steve had a fine voice, and so did Miss Hungerford, and the songs got to be like duets between those two, with the other pupils piping away in the background.

After assembly, classes began. There weren't enough seats to go around, so Miss Hungerford always gave somebody her chair and stood up all day. She taught every subject: French, German, algebra, history, English. She always gave her pupils the feeling that she learned with them. "Tell me about the Battle of Lake Erie," she'd say. "I'm curious to know."

Miss Hungerford started the Hawthorne and the Whittier literary clubs, where the boys and girls talked about authors and had ice cream afterward. Sometimes, during refreshments, she would talk about "etiquette." She would say, "Now, Stephen Pigott, suppose you were invited to a formal dinner. How would you greet your hostess?"

"She's a *dedicated* sort of woman," people said, watching her walk back and forth from her boardinghouse to the school, early and late, in a shirtwaist and skirt and a little stiff hat, always with a load of books on her arm. She went to church twice on Sundays and to prayer meeting Wednesday nights. But she never said a word about religion, except for that sentence on the blackboard. She just sort of lived it.

Everyone has wondered since just what there was about Miss Hungerford that fired her pupils so. Somehow she made them believe they lived in a fine world, where a miracle could happen any morning, and they were fortunate and wonderful, with a lot of talent. "We've never thought so well of ourselves since," the

Cornwall people say. And she sent out from that school a batch of youngsters who became important men and women all over the country.

Miss Hungerford took trouble with everybody, but she worked hardest with Steve. He stayed on in high school. She told him over and over that books were important; they were doors. Steve began wondering if there might be a door for him. Especially the spring of his senior year, when they were reading "The Vision of Sir Launfal."

"A vision is a dream," Miss Hungerford told him one night after school while he was clapping chalk dust out of the blackboard erasers. "My dream is always to stay with boys and girls and books. What is yours, Stephen?"

He said to her then what he'd never said to a living soul: "I want to be—a marine engineer."

He thought she'd laugh, but she sat there with her eyes sparkling. "You *can* be a marine engineer," she said. "All you need is the will to do it."

She had to give him faith in himself little by little. When she finally got Steve to speak to his father about going to college, Pat Pigott said Steve was crazy. Miss Hungerford was stubborn, though, and when fall came Steve went to Columbia University to take the mechanical engineering course.

He earned his way by working in a trolley barn; he sang in a church choir for five dollars a Sunday, and did all sorts of odd jobs, studying whenever he could. Every time he got to thinking he ought to give the whole thing up, he'd slip away to Cornwall, and Miss Hungerford would somehow pour courage into him.

Stephen Pigott was president of the class in his junior year; he edited the engineering-school publication; he sang in the university glee club; he was elected to a Greek-letter fraternity. And when he graduated in 1903, Miss Hungerford sent him a telegram: *"I told you so."*

In 1908, Steve went to Scotland to help install a Curtis turbine for John Brown & Company, Ltd., the big shipbuilding firm that built the *Mauritania* and the *Lusitania*. He had planned to remain only four months, but the company persuaded him to stay on.

In 1938, he became managing director of the company. He had designed the machinery for more than three hundred British ships: cruisers, submarines, the *Hood,* the *Duke of York,* the *Queen Mary.*

During these thirty years Steve and Miss Hungerford kept up their friendship, writing to each other almost every week.

On the *Queen Mary's* maiden voyage Steve came back to America for a few days. Columbia was giving him an honorary degree; the American Society of Mechanical Engineers was awarding him a medal.

When he went to Cornwall the whole town turned out to meet him, and he made a speech in the big new high school. Everyone expected him to talk about his work, or the fine people he had met abroad. But what he talked about was Miss Hungerford.

"Few men have been blessed with a friendship such as she has given to me for nearly half a century," he said. "When I have felt pride in any accomplished work, the things she said to me have been in my heart."

Miss Hungerford was now teaching in an upstate town near the shore of Lake Ontario. When Steve telephoned to say that he was coming to see her, he was told she was seriously ill, and was advised not to make the visit. And so he had to sail without seeing her.

Steve is Sir Stephen Pigott now—he was knighted in 1939,

about the time he designed the machinery for the *Queen Elizabeth.*

Miss Hungerford, now eighty-five, is still living in her upstate town, where she had kept on working until she was almost eighty. A few years ago, her town dedicated to her the Frances Irene Hungerford Library, "in appreciation of her fineness of character, her devotion to her work, and the lasting impression she has made."

That was the story they told me in Cornwall. It made me wonder what it was about Miss Hungerford that had made people remember her all their lives. So, a few weeks ago, I went upstate to spend a day with her.

She came running down the front steps to meet me, light as a feather. Her hair is snow-white, but her eyes are the same deep blue. Even after what the Cornwall people had told me, I was not prepared for how tiny she is. Or how radiantly alive.

Her home is like her: tiny, cheerful, neat as a new pin. She showed me all over it, moving with quick, firm steps like a girl. In the book-filled sitting room I sat in her Boston rocker while she talked to me about Sir Stephen. She had newspaper clippings, pictures, Christmas cards, fifty years of his letters.

But, though I tried all day, I couldn't get Miss Hungerford to talk about herself. She was willing to tell only about her old pupils, calling each one by name. We had high tea at her grandmother's fine old table, and she asked a blessing. We spoke of how Sir Stephen had promised to come to see her when the war is over, of how he had written in his last letter: "Wait for me, Miss Hungerford."

"I hope," she said, "that I can live long enough to see Stephen again."

"Why, Miss Hungerford," I said, "you'll live forever!"

"I know that," she answered gravely, "but I may soon be out of touch with all you people for a little while."

When the car came for me, we walked to the curb together, her hand laid lightly on my arm. And then, for the first time, she spoke about herself. "You know, I feel ashamed," she said, "when I see all these bright modern teachers. Compared to them, I was not very well trained." She paused; her hand tightened on my arm. "You see, all I had was *love.*"

Dorothy Walworth
(1900–1953)

of Cornwall, New York, also wrote such books as *Faith of Our Fathers, The Pride of the Town, Chickens Come Home to Roost, Rainbow at Noon,* and *Nicodemus.*

PINKY

Mabel Beaton

*P*inky was his brother—but not his real brother—and
he always treated him accordingly. Pinky was such a pest!
  Why couldn't he look for friends elsewhere!
  Years later, Pinky did just that. Then Ralph wondered
if it was too late to undo the coldness of those years.

inky, of course, was only a stepbrother to Ralph Henwood. There was no tie of blood to make him tender toward the little chap. When Mrs. Henwood had married Mr. Davis, Pinky's father, six-year-old Ralph had looked the two-year-old boy over with a critical and unfriendly eye. The boy, all pink and white, suggested but one thing to Ralph—a shy, white rabbit—and he promptly nicknamed him "Pinky."

The name held, too. In time, even Mrs. Davis took it up, so that his earlier name was all but forgotten.

Pinky, for all his soft whiteness, was a sturdy little fellow. He followed Ralph about the place, and endeavored, in his baby way, to keep up with the interests of the older boy.

"Isn't it nice to have a little brother?" Mrs. Davis said to Ralph at times.

But Ralph never committed himself. "I—don't know," he hesitated. "He's too little."

"He'll grow," smiled the mother. "Some day he'll be a lot of company for you."

"He tags after me all the time. I wish he wouldn't," Ralph murmured under his breath.

But if Mrs. Davis caught the rebellious whisper, she wisely did not appear to.

Ralph can't help coming to love him, she thought to herself.

Months passed, and still little Pinky tagged continuously at Ralph's heels, and he still continued to be snubbed by the older boy.

"If something would happen to draw the boys together, I should be perfectly happy," said Mrs. Davis to her husband. "There's enough difference in their dispositions to make them good friends, and they ought to mean a great deal to each other. But Ralph is always off with other boys."

"Never mind," Mr. Davis cheered her, "these things always take time. In a few years the difference in their ages will not seem so great. Their living together daily will form a stronger tie than you realize. By the time Ralph is fourteen, you will see they will be the brothers that you want them to be."

Mrs. Davis dropped the subject, but not because she was entirely convinced. She saw more of the boys than did Mr. Davis, and the closest observance failed to bring to light any signs of their growing nearer to each other.

By the time Ralph was ten, he was carelessly superior in his treatment of Pinky. Pinky, never harboring a suspicion that Ralph was slighting him, trudged to school after the older boy, with the same dogged devotion and admiration he had shown since his baby days.

"Help Pinky with his lessons, dear," Mrs. Davis often suggested. But Ralph was ready with an excuse, reasonable or unreasonable.

If she urged still further, he fell back upon an old line of reasoning that he would know his lessons better if he worked them out alone. "Our teacher tells us that, and I guess he knows."

"But a little help over the hard places means a good deal to a beginner. I used to help you, you know."

"But Pinky learns very much easier than I did, Mother."

It was true. Pinky, perhaps from his loneliness and lack of aid, mastered lessons far beyond his years. By the time Ralph was fourteen, Pinky had cut the difference between them to two years, as far as standing in school was concerned.

Ralph had done well, too. At fourteen he entered the

Academy twenty miles away, which necessitated his being away from home.

Mrs. Davis worried over that. "I know Ralph is a good boy, and I am not afraid to trust him. But—"

"But what?"

"I know you will laugh when I say I would really feel safer if Pinky were with him. Pinky is the younger, I know, but there is something about him—"

"Without a doubt, Pinky would keep close at Ralph's heels. Well, why can't we send him? Your sister could keep two boys as easily as one. There's a good church school in the city."

"But the expense—"

"Don't think of that. I am sure I shall not, where the good of our two boys is concerned. And if Pinky's going will make you feel easier, he shall go, of course."

"Yes, it would greatly relieve me."

"Then Pinky shall go. Let's tell him now. It will please him, all right."

Pinky indeed showed great delight when the change was announced. He could hardly wait while arrangements were being made.

"I can go right away, can't I?" he asked. "I don't have to wait till Monday, do I? I'd like to go and surprise Ralph."

"Don't you think it would be nicer to wait and go with Ralph, when he comes home at the end of the week?"

But Pinky shook his head.

"Today's only Tuesday. Please, please, let me go tomorrow and surprise him. It will be the surprise of his life to find I am to be there, too."

Mr. and Mrs. Davis talked it over and decided to let Pinky have his way.

"He doesn't have many good times, poor little fellow!" Mrs. Davis said. "And doubtless Ralph will be only too glad to have someone from home with him."

But if Ralph was glad when Pinky arrived, he managed to conceal the fact exceedingly well. Pinky's face fell at his cool reception.

"If you don't want me—," he began.

"Oh, it's all right," Ralph said carelessly. "The schools are better here, and you'll get along faster, but don't expect to see much of me. I'm in the Academy now, you know, and the fellows I go with aren't keen on grammar school boys."

"But who'll I go with?"

"You'll find plenty of boys in your own class. I see them every day. Your school is next to mine."

"But—I wanted to be near you."

"You'll be near enough," Ralph said irritably. *Too near!* he added to himself.

Pinky never stayed despondent for any length of time. He brightened now at a sudden thought. "There are all the nights!" he cried. "I'll have you to myself then, won't I?"

"Well, I rather guess not!" Ralph said hastily; "I have to prepare my lessons then."

"But after you get through with them, there'll be lots of time. We can talk after we're in bed, can't we?"

"I don't see how, with the doors shut."

"Can't I sleep with you?"

"No."

"Why? I saw two beds in your room."

"There *were* two, but I asked Aunt Mary to take one out."

Pinky said no more. His disappointment was keen, but he kept it inside.

He started in the new school the following day. The work was harder than it had been at home, and for a time he was occupied solely with keeping up with the class. But by degrees the work became familiar and easy to him, and he began to find time heavy on his hands.

"What shall I do after school, Ralph?" he asked. "Can't we go somewhere, just the two of us?"

"No, we can't. I'm busy enough with my work. Find some of the boys, and go around with them."

"But—"

Ralph turned at the odd tremble in the word. Pinky's eyes appealed to him, and the older boy half hesitated.

"I just can't, Pinky," he said. "I would if I could, but the other fellows wouldn't want a fellow of your age hanging around. Find your own chums. You used to be a friendly chap back home."

"But these boys seem so different."

"Oh, well, you'll get used to them in time. Run away now, and don't bother me."

Pinky went out slowly. He did not turn at the door and look back with the little crooked smile to which Ralph was so accustomed. He did not leave the door partly ajar, as if he expected to come again soon. Instead, he closed it, and with an air of finality.

Now he's huffed! Ralph thought. *I'm sure I don't care. I only hope he'll stay that way, and leave me entirely alone.*

As time went on, Ralph found that Pinky was following his suggestion. Pinky's school was dismissed an hour before Ralph was free, but he was not waiting around the corner for Ralph to walk home with him. Nor did he come up the stairs, three steps at a time, if Ralph missed him and reached home first.

I'm glad he has found a way of amusing himself, Ralph thought, *without having to pester me all the time.*

Apparently Pinky had. Ralph looked at him sometimes as they sat at the dinner table as if he saw him for the first time. There was something new about his face—something puzzling; whether pleasing or not, Ralph could not quite decide.

Pinky looks different, he thought. *He has found his bearings, and will get along all right now.*

Aunt Mary noticed the change, too. She watched Pinky with shrewd, kindly eyes. *That boy is up to mischief of some sort,* she said to herself. *Sister said he was as steady as a clock. I thought so myself when he first came, but he has not a steady look any longer. He never meets your eyes if he can help it. When I get a chance I must speak to Ralph about him.*

The chance was not long in coming. There was no longer any danger of Pinky's happening in; he was in the house only when he was obliged to be.

Aunt Mary dropped into a chair by Ralph's littered table. "Ralph," she asked, "what's the matter with Pinky?"

Ralph held his finger in his book as he answered. "Oh, nothing, I guess, Aunt Mary," he said carelessly.

"Do you mean to say that you can't see any change in him?"

Ralph searched back through a mind as littered as his table, trying to find the image of Pinky therein.

"Why," he replied, "I believe he is a bit changed. He's growing up, you see. When he came here he was only a little white rabbit."

Aunt Mary sighed again. "He will be a black one the first thing you know, or I miss my guess. He is into mischief, and I know it. I have had much experience with boys, and I know most of the signs."

"I guess not. I don't know what he could get into."

"You ought to find out," Aunt Mary went on. "It is your job

to look out for your brother. Just have a good talk with him, and find out what has gone wrong."

"I will when I get a chance," Ralph promised.

"Don't be too long finding a chance," cautioned Aunt Mary, as she left the room.

Ralph thought of Pinky more than once that afternoon. There was something new and strange about the boy. And yet if there was anything wrong with him, they would have noticed it at home.

Aunt Mary just imagines things, he summed it up at last. *If Pinky had been changed any, who would have seen it more quickly than Mother? Mother would have noticed right away. However, I will have a heart-to-heart talk with Pinky one of these days. There are some pretty bad boys at that school, and it's just as well to put Pinky on his guard.*

The intention, though, was as far as it went with Ralph. His work at school was interesting and engrossing. In his leisure time he had his own friends and his own pleasures. There really was no place for Pinky and his troubles.

But I'll do it some day, Ralph promised himself.

Then suddenly he found it was too late. He was called to the telephone in school one day. Aunt Mary's voice, strained and strange, bade him come home at once. Ralph was white-lipped by the time he reached the house.

Aunt Mary broke the news without preamble: "There is no good beating about the bush," she said. "Pinky is in trouble. He has written to me."

"To you?"

There was a hint of hurt in Ralph's voice.

"To me, of course. To whom else would the poor boy write? He sent only a few lines, but—"

"Why didn't he come instead of writing?"

"Come! He couldn't. *He is in jail.*"

Ralph sank into a chair and covered his face with his hands.

Aunt Mary eyed him with the pity of one who has known regret. "Don't feel hard toward him," she began. "He is not altogether to blame. I warned you to go right down and see him. I do not know what he has done, but whatever it is, we are going to stand right by him. Go right down now. And—don't be hard on him, Ralph."

Ralph groaned. How little Aunt Mary understood the thoughts that were hammering in his brain—the regret, the pity, the love, the brotherhood! Ralph knew that by the sudden rush of tears to his eyes.

Down in the jail he found little Pinky, white-faced and miserable, with no longer a claim to the old name. He gave Ralph no greeting, made no explanation, but sat in stubborn silence, his eyes on the floor.

Ralph was obliged to leave him at last, and ask information of the police sergeant at the desk. The man was kindly and talkative. A till had been robbed. Three of the boys, two of whom were old offenders, had been caught.

"Very likely that little fellow you have come to see just happened to fall in with bad company. I do not believe he had a thing to do with it. It will all come out when the others confess. Oh, yes, they are pretty certain to. The captain has a way of making them own up."

Ralph steadied his lips at last to ask a question. "Could I—could I just stay there in place of him tonight? He'll be afraid. He's so—little."

"Why, no," said the kindly sergeant, "you couldn't do that. But bail will be accepted, of course. Let's see what it will be."

An hour later Ralph went in to tell Pinky of his liberty,

temporary liberty at least. Pinky still sat in sullen solitude. He did not turn at the opening of the door. Ralph fell on his knees beside him.

"Pinky!" he cried. "Brother!"

Pinky threw off his hand. "You were ashamed of me before," he said; "how will you feel now?"

"But, Pinky, I'm not ashamed of you. I'm ashamed of myself. *I* am the one who ought to be in jail. If it comes to a trial, I'll tell my story to the judge, and perhaps he'll punish me instead of you. It's all my fault."

He put his arm around Pinky again, and this time the younger brother did not draw away. Ralph held him closer. A love that was almost fierce welled up in his heart, and he longed to protect him, to do battle for him against the whole world. There was not much he could say now, but he could *show* his love from now on!

"Come, Brother; come on home with me."

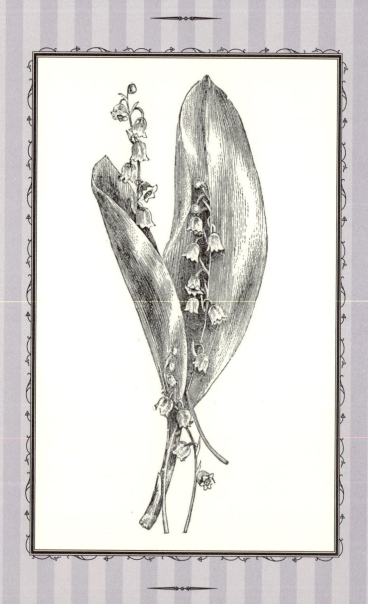

THANK YOU,
ROSIE

Arthur A. Milward

*O*h, *how often we pigeonhole people according to their relative respectability. By such a measuring device, many of us would have turned the other way had Rosie approached us—for Rosie, like Mary Magdalene, was a woman with a dubious reputation.*

But beneath her scarlet profession . . . beat a heart as big as old London itself, and she taught him the meaning of true friendship.

t had been a long, long year—the last year of my son Adrian's brief life. The journey up by train to London's Waterloo Station had become almost routine. Then the twenty-five-minute walk across Waterloo Bridge and on to the Hospital for Sick Children, Great Ormond Street. The walk to the hospital was not without enjoyment, for I was eager to see my son again and buoyed up by the somehow indestructible hope that today, by some miracle, he would be recovering.

But the return to the railway station in the evening was devastating. Once again, no miracle. Some evenings it became, as the French say, *insupportable*.

After putting my little son to bed in the ward, hearing his prayers and holding him in my arms while he fell asleep, I usually had plenty of time to make my way to the railway station. I frequently paused on the bridge spanning the River Thames to watch the broad river flowing along on its never-ending journey to the sea.

One evening I gazed, hypnotized almost, into the black, oily water and was not immediately aware that a woman had joined me. I looked up and saw her; she was standing quite close. I had seen her before in the shadows on the opposite side of the street and had recognized, without giving the matter much thought, that she was, almost certainly, of the sisterhood euphemistically referred to as "ladies of the evening."

"Evenin', Guv'nor," she said.

"Good evening," I replied, a little discomfited by her presence and unsure of her intentions.

She looked into the Thames. "You been to the Children's," she said. It was a statement rather than a question.

"Yes, I have," I told her, a bit bewildered by her interest. "My little son is a patient there."

"Bad, ain't he?" she said.

"Yes, I'm afraid he is," I replied. And again, as much to myself as to her, "I'm very much afraid he is."

She reached out and touched my arm. I could see tears in her eyes. "I'm sorry, Guv," she said softly. Then she withdrew her hand quickly, turned, and walked away. I thought about the encounter all the way home and felt strangely heartened by it.

For the next few months, I regularly made my way to and from the children's hospital, my emotions alternating wildly between unreasoning hope and complete despair. Often she would join me on the bridge.

"'Ow is 'e, then?" she would inquire. "Anything different? 'E's in Mr. Punch Ward, ain't 'e?"

"Yes, he is," I agreed, wondering how she knew. "There's no change."

She never asked my name but she invited me to call her Rosie. "That's what me friends call me."

"My son's name is Adrian, Rosie," I told her. "He's quite blond with gray eyes, and he's almost four years old."

She nodded and said nothing.

I came to rely on these encounters to a remarkable degree and one evening gave her a small picture of Adrian, a duplicate of one I carried in my billfold. I wrote on the back of it: "Thank you, Rosie." She looked at it for a long moment before wrapping it in her handkerchief and putting it carefully in her purse.

Then, finally, the telephone call came from the children's hospital: "I think you had better come at once."

He looked so small lying there, his gray eyes fixed earnestly on mine. I leaned over and wiped the perspiration from his forehead.

"Daddy, why are you crying? Daddy, I'm frightened. Oh, Daddy, is it going to be all right?"

"Yes, darling, Daddy's here. It's going to be all right." The tiny hand clasped in mine relaxed its grip. When it was over, the two compassionate nurses put their arms around my shoulders and led me away.

I went out into the London streets—and it was night.

The following evening, after taking care of necessary business at the hospital, I stopped on the bridge and leaned over the railings, gazing, unseeing, into the water, trying to get a grip on myself. When I turned, Rosie was standing beside me. She touched me gently on the arm, just as she had the first time we met.

"'Ere," she said, proffering me something wrapped in white tissue paper. "They're for 'im. You'll put 'em on 'is grave for me, won't you?" Thrusting a tiny bouquet of lilies of the valley into my hand, she made a sort of choking sound, turned and ran.

A mass of wreaths covered the grave. In the center of the profusion of floral tributes the tiny bunch of lilies of the valley contrasted sharply with the vivid roses, daffodils, tulips and anemones that surrounded it.

I timed my return from my final visit to the hospital vicinity so that I would pass by Waterloo Bridge rather late in the evening. I wanted to tell Rosie that I had delivered her flowers. But I saw nothing of her. I could not imagine what had happened to her.

Summoning up my courage, I made my way to the nearest police station, not many blocks distant. With the unfailing courtesy and genuine helpfulness of the British policeman, an officer listened to my story of looking for a friend. He eyed me a bit quizzically.

"Yes, sir, I am almost sure I know to whom you refer," he assured me. "She was regularly in the vicinity of Waterloo Bridge. Her regular 'beat,' you might say. Her name was Rosie, wasn't it?"

"Yes, sir," I said. "That's the person I'm looking for."

"I'm sorry, sir," he told me quietly. "The person in question is dead. We picked her up in the street several nights ago. Apparently a heart attack."

"Did she have any relatives, any family?" I asked.

"No, sir, I'm sorry," the policeman said. "We went through her purse, but there was no identification of any kind. Cosmetics, matches, cigarettes, handkerchief, a couple of pictures. That was all."

"Do you still have her purse?" I asked. "Would it be possible for me to see it—to look into it?"

The officer hesitated. "Well, sir, that's rather an unusual request."

"Look, officer," I continued, taking out my billfold and withdrawing the picture of my son from it. "This is my son. If the person you picked up is really the one I'm looking for, there will be an identical picture in her purse."

"Just a moment, sir," the officer said and retreated to an inner office. Within minutes he returned, carrying a brown purse with a large card attached, evidently a listing of the purse's contents. He looked excited.

"Yes, sir," he assured me, running his finger down the list on the card. "There are two snapshots in the purse."

He opened the purse and handed me two photographs. One was a replica of the picture I held in my hand. I turned it over and read in my own handwriting: "Thank you, Rosie." The other picture was of a small, dark-haired girl.

I had one more place to go. The following day I took the train to London and made my way to the children's hospital. I recalled Rosie mentioning that she had a friend "Ben," who was a porter at the hospital. I inquired at the porters' lodge. A middle-aged man with a kindly face came forward.

"Yes, indeed," he assured me. "I knew Rosie. She used to stop by regularly, you know, and inquire about your boy. I used to get a report for her from the ward about him.

"She wasn't always in the line of business she was in when you met her, you know," Ben continued. "She used to be a waitress. It was after she lost her girl she went on the street. The little girl died in here, you know, six years old. It was about a year ago. That's when I first met Rosie—she used to come here and visit Gerda. That was the child's name. After the little one died, Rosie never went back to the waitress job."

"Ben, can you tell me where Rosie is buried?"

"No, Guv, I can't," Ben said. "But I can tell you where the child lies. Rosie used to go there every Sunday afternoon and cut the grass and take flowers. I went with her a time or two."

I knelt beside the tiny mound. Lacking shears, I tried to pull the longest grass, growing lank and weedy now, with my hands. I filled the blue vase with water from the faucet in the corner of the cemetery and replaced it on the grave.

Unwrapping the tissue paper from the small bouquet I carried, I placed the lilies of the valley in the vase, thrust the paper in the pocket of my raincoat, rose from my knees, and walked rapidly away.

Arthur Milward

living in Kennett Square, Pennsylvania, is a professional freelance writer (a number of his stories, including this one, have been featured in *Reader's Digest*). Milward remembers days and nights etched in almost insupportable anguish, for his small son, Adrian, who lay dying in London's Hospital for Sick Children. And he remembers, too, just as clearly, Rosie.

A DARLING

Ernest Gilmore

The word darling *can mean many things. Like the protean word* love, *its elasticity makes it almost meaningless. Yet in this very old story a father labeled his daughter a "darling"—but was it the truth or mere parental prejudice?*

wo gentlemen, friends who had been parted for years, met in a crowded city thoroughfare. The one who lived in the city was on his way to meet a pressing business engagement. After a few expressions of delight, he said: "Well, I'm off. I'm sorry, but it can't be helped. I will look for you tomorrow at dinner. Remember, two o'clock sharp. I'm anxious for you to see my wife and child."

"Only one?" asked the other.

"Only one," came the answer, tenderly, "a daughter. She's a darling, I do assure you."

And then they parted, the stranger in the city getting into a streetcar bound for the park, whither he desired to go.

After a block or two a group of five girls entered the car. They were all young, and evidently belonged to families of wealth and culture—that is, intellectual culture—as they conversed well. Each carried an elaborately decorated lunch basket; each was attired in a becoming spring suit. Doubtless they were going to the park for a spring picnic. They seemed very happy and amiable until the car stopped, this time letting in a pale-faced girl of about eleven and a sick boy of four. These children were shabbily dressed, and upon their faces there were looks of distress mingled with some expectancy. Were they, too, on their way to the park? The gentleman thought so; so did the group of girls, for he heard one of them say, with a look of disdain, "I suppose those raga-muffins are on an excursion, too."

"I shouldn't want to leave my door if I had to look like that. Should you?" This from another girl.

"No, indeed; but there is no accounting for tastes. I think there ought to be a special line of cars for the lower classes."

All this conversation went on in a low tone, but the gentleman heard it. Had the little girl, too? He glanced at her pale face, and saw tears glistening in her eyes. Then he looked at the group of finely dressed girls, who had moved as far from the plebeians as the limits of the car would allow. He was angry. With difficulty, he resisted telling them that they were vain and heartless as they drew their costly trappings closer about them, as if fearful of contact with poverty's children.

Just then an exclamation: "Why, there's Nettie! Wonder where she is going?" caused him to look out where, on the corner, a sweet-faced young girl stood waiting for the car. When she entered, she was warmly greeted by the five, and they made room for her beside them. They were profuse in their exclamations and questions.

"Where are you going?" asked one.

"Oh, what lovely flowers! Whom are they for?" questioned another.

"I'm on my way to Belle Clark's. She's sick, you know, and the flowers are for her."

She answered both questions at once, and then, glancing toward the door, she saw the pale girl looking wistfully at her. She smiled at the child, a tender look beaming from her beautiful eyes; and then, forgetting that she, too, wore a handsome velvet skirt and costly jacket, and that her shapely hands were covered with well-fitting gloves, she left her seat and crossed over to the little ones. Laying one hand caressingly on the boy's thin cheek, she asked his sister: "The little boy is sick, is he not? And he is your brother, I am sure, he clings so to you?"

It seemed hard for the girl to answer, but finally she said: "Yes, miss; he is sick. Freddy never has been well. Yes, miss; he is my brother. We're goin' to the park, to see if 'twon't make Freddy better."

"I am glad you are going," the young girl replied, in a low

voice meant for no ears but those of the child addressed. "I feel sure it will do him good. It is lovely there, with the spring flowers all in bloom. But where is your lunch? You ought to have a lunch after so long a ride."

Over the girl's face came a flush. "Yes, miss, mebbe we ought to, for Freddy's sake; but you see we didn't have any lunch to bring. Tim—he's our brother—he saved these pennies on purpose so Freddy could ride to the park and back. I guess Freddy'll forget about being hungry when he gets to the beautiful park."

Were there tears in the lovely girl's eyes as she listened? Yes, there certainly were; and very soon she asked the child where they lived, and wrote the address down in a tablet which she took from a beaded bag upon her arm.

After riding a few blocks the pretty girl left the car, but she had not left the little ones comfortless. Half the bouquet of violets and hyacinths was clasped in the sister's hand, while the sick boy, with radiant face, held a precious package, from which he helped himself now and then, saying to his sister in a jubilant whisper: "She said we could eat 'em all—every one—when we got to the park. What made her so sweet and good to us? She didn't call us ragamuffins, and wasn't 'fraid to have her dress touch ours; and she called me a 'dear,' she did. What made her?"

And Sue whispered back: "I guess it's 'cause she's beautiful as well as her clothes—beautiful *inside,* you know."

The gentleman's ears served him well. He heard Sue's whisper, and thought: *Yes, the child is right; the lovely young girl* is *beautiful inside—beautiful in spirit. She is one of the Lord's own, developing in Christian growth. Bless her!*

At two o'clock sharp the next day the two gentlemen, as agreed, met again.

"This is my wife," the host said, proudly introducing a comely lady; "and this," as a young girl of fifteen entered the parlor, "is my daughter, Nettie."

Ah, thought the guest as he extended his hand in cordial greeting, *this is the dear girl whom I met yesterday in the streetcar. I don't wonder her father calls her a darling. She is a darling, and no mistake, bless her!*

BLUE RIBBON

Author Unknown

*O*nly nine years old and an orphan. Then Mary Callender took him to her farm, and to her heart. Friendship with her salvaged his childhood, friendship with golden-haired Sally gave him something to strive toward, and friendship with the young horse gave him something to love.

e was glad, big Peter Carlin was, that there was no plane service to the remote spot where he was going, no train that would get him there in time. Glad because it meant that he could have this eight-hour drive alone; and today, of all days, he wanted to be alone. He wanted to think, undisturbed; and as the car hummed its way into the first of the three hundred miles, his thoughts went back and back, to the very beginning, to the real reason why he was making this trip and what it meant to him. Back to the day, twenty years ago, when he had been only nine, and Mary Callender had come to take him home. To her home.

A small boy he had been then, on that late-spring morning, small but straight of back and shoulder, wiry in his slender arms and legs, his blue overalls washed and rewashed to a faded blue that was lighter even than his eyes—eyes that had been red-rimmed by morning, red-rimmed because he had dug at them all through the night with grimy little paws that no one had made him wash. He wouldn't cry. Big boys of nine didn't cry, not even when they fell off hayracks or had their faces switched sharp by cows' ropy tails at milking time.

His father had told him that—never to cry. And he wouldn't. But it wasn't easy, sitting there in Mrs. Sylvester's rocking-chaired parlor, hearing the voices through the kitchen door, wondering what was going to happen and feeling so bewildered and frightened, so very alone.

"It's a shame, that's what it is," Mrs. Sylvester was saying. "First his mother four years ago, and now his father. And so sudden, too. Just a cold, it started out to be. And now the poor little fellow with no home and no relatives that anybody ever heard tell of. I'd take him myself, if there was room."

And then Mary Callender's voice, very strong and deep, but

very gentle. He had always liked Mary Callender. "But I want to take him. I really do. He'll be company for me, and a help, too, running the place. He knows already how things should be done. Where is he now?"

And he had stood up quickly, pretending to be looking at the geraniums in their tin coffee cans on the window ledge, trying to keep his upper lip steady as Mary Callender came in.

"Good morning, Peter," she had said, as if he were her own age. "How would you like to slide up to my place for a while and give me a hand with things? There's lots of hay to get down, and I can use another man on the hayrake and driving the loader team."

Things that she knew he liked to do, working with horses.

⟐

She understood, Mary Callender did. There weren't many things that she didn't understand. Older than his father, she was, with iron-gray hair and eyes that were blue, too, like Peter's only deep-set under heavy eyebrows and with friendly little lines at their corners because she liked to smile.

Her mouth was friendly, too, but strong; her skin rich-colored from the sun and weather, but still soft; her hands rough-knotted from the work that she had known for so many years. Life hadn't been easy for Mary Callender, but it hadn't left her hard. There was a gentleness, a tenderness, that small Peter could only sense, that drew him to her—a haven, a home.

He didn't speak, not quite trusting that, but he nodded, and again she understood.

"Fine," she said heartily. "I've got a team outside. Why don't you just throw your gear into the back seat and we'll get off?" Adding, with a quick gleam to her clear eyes: "Got a surprise for you, too, down at the barn."

And when his suitcase, cracked and cardboard, was in and he had said good-bye to Mrs. Sylvester, Mary Callender said casually, "Guess you'd better handle 'em, Peter; they're a mite skittish this morning," offering him the reins as he braced one small foot against the whip socket, the way his father had done, and swung the team of bays out into the road. That was the first time then, that moment, that he had forgotten the ache, dull and deep inside, forgotten, if only for a moment, those last four days. There was a slight stir of interest, even, in his mind for what this new surprise might be.

It was five miles up to Mary Callender's hill farm, to the four hundred acres that she owned and ran, five miles uphill through fields where the billowing hay caught at the wheelspokes, and the team of bays nipped out for hasty mouthfuls. Peter had been there before, of course, and he liked the old gray-shingled house, white-trimmed, with the bell on the roof and the kittens always playing around the dooryard under the giant, leafy rustling maples. It was all so comfortable, so secure, with the red barns just over the brow of the hill and the brook below. The best farm in the county, maybe in the state, his father had always said; the best run, too, even if a woman did run it.

His room was to be just over the kitchen, with its scrubbed white floor, its stone sink and the separator rings drying over the wood range. "It'll be nice and warm up there in the winter," Mary Callender had said, and when he had unpacked his things he came down and waited shyly.

"Doughnut pail's in the pantry," Mary Callender told him. "You get a fresh one and then I want you should come down to the barn. Something there I think you'll like." And, munching on a bit of feathery crispness, he followed her down and into the horse barn, his step quickened by the wonder of what could be waiting there.

Cattle were Mary Callender's business, milk for the city three hundred miles away her livelihood, and she had eighty Jerseys, soft-eyed, sleek and quick as deer, rich milkers, purebreds all. *But horses were her love,* her real love, the pride and joy that had made the work, the struggle and the worry of running her farm, worthwhile over the years.

Horses she knew, through and through, fetlock to forelock, and they knew her, too; understood her and trusted her. They would do things for her hand, light on the reins, and for her voice, kindly but firm, that others could never get out of them.

Not always the best horses, because that meant money—money which Mary Callender did not have. Even the stock she had kept her poor—bleakly poor at times, although she never spoke of it; but there was always a sparkling light span for the red-wheeled gig in the summer and the sleigh in winter, and usually five or six work horses, fat and sleek and powerful.

But sometimes there was a horse like the Gray Lady, before whose box stall Mary Callender stopped now with small Peter. Purebred, the Gray Lady was, every inch of her, purebred Arabian, with the sharp ears, the forehead slightly concave, the wide, sensitive nostrils and the tail that was a flowing plume. Dapple gray and flamingly alive, perfect but for one thing: she was *blind*.

Her owner had imported her, and then, when her eyes had suddenly failed, he had come to Mary Callender. "Take her," he said. "She'll have good care with you, and perhaps she can have a sound colt. Maybe crossed with a Thoroughbred stallion."

So Mary had taken her gladly, never thinking of extra feed bills, extra care, content only to sit for hours when she could, watching the effortless grace, the easy rhythm of the gray mare as she circled the paddock that she grew to know by instinct. At first it had clutched at Mary Callender's heart, seeing the animal blunder blindly into the padded fenceposts, but soon the horse had learned the boundaries, sensing the final second when she must stop her flight.

And now, in the box stall beside the Gray Lady, was her first colt, sound of eye and body, with the same gray dapplings, long and leggy with a mop brush for a tail and a colt's soft woolly fur. Three months old it was on that day when small Peter had first seen it, holding out his hand for a soft, warm nuzzle from the velvety, inquisitive nose.

"Isn't he a beauty?" she said at last, and Peter nodded again, but with a quick smile, a quick look that brought one of Mary Callender's arms around his shoulder, sensing as she did the love that he had for these creatures, a love as great as her own.

Then, after a long pause, she spoke again. "He likes you, too, Peter." Slowly: "You're new here, too, both of you; but you're going to be happy, too, I hope. Would you like"—so very wisely—"would you like to have this colt for your own? To train and ride and handle, to care for?"

And small Peter's eyes, wide now, and not quite believing, went quickly up to hers. "You mean—you mean that he'd be mine? *All mine?*" And Mary Callender nodded.

"Gee" the whisper straight from his heart—"Gee, would I!" The dullness, the loneliness gone suddenly from his face, not to return till late that evening when he was in his bed and thoughts were to come back. Thoughts that brought stifling tears and finally Mary Callender to soothe them, so comforting, so reassuring as if she had been with her own son.

⟢⟢•⟣⟣

He remembered all that, big Peter did, remembered it as if it were yesterday, driving home again along the road that he knew so well, his lean, brown hands tightening on the wheel as the memories flooded back.

They had grown up together through those two years, the gray colt and the boy, grown up together closely side by side, until they knew each other better, almost, than two people ever could. "Gray Boy, I think I'll call him," Peter had said, "if it's all right"; and Mary Callender thought it was all right.

She loved to watch them together, the colt tall and long-barreled now, deep of shoulder, with a crinkly forelock over its eyes, following Peter everywhere about the farm, whinnying eagerly at the barnyard gate when Peter had been away. A clean-limbed animal the young horse was, powerful but quick-wheeling, graceful as a barn swallow.

And everything, every bit of care, Peter gave the horse himself. No one else could even bed it down at night. He fed it, Peter did, groomed and brushed and combed it until Mary Callender laughed and warned him that he would wear its coat away; broke it to shelter, and then, when it was just over two, he began working it for the saddle.

First with a blanket thrown loosely over his back. Next, a girth strap, and finally just two years from the time that he had come to Mary's, Peter put on a saddle. An old army saddle that had been in the attic storeroom for years, scarred and dusty, its box stirrups warped and cracked, all far beyond the aid of the oil and saddle soap that he rubbed in so painstakingly, so hopefully.

Mary had held the Gray Boy firmly by the bridle the first time that Peter had swung up onto its back. But there had been no need. The horse quivered slightly for just a second; then its fine head came around, its keen eyes peering up and back at Peter as if questioning the reason for all this. Then, satisfied, ears sharply pricked, mane flowing, they were off across the meadow and along the brook, swinging back finally to a stop at Mary's side.

"He's wonderful," Peter said, face flushed with pride, "just like a rocking chair, and smooth as flying."

And Mary nodded. "He is beautiful to watch," she said, thinking that they both were. "In a little while you can teach him gaits."

That was the beginning, that first day, the beginning of a new bond between them, the gray horse with the rickety saddle and the small boy in blue overalls, soon familiar sights for miles around, cantering the dusty roads, cutting across the meadowlands. It was not until almost fall that Peter discovered that the horse loved to jump, and after that they never looked for gates or bridges, taking small brooks, stone walls and fallen trees with an easy grace, sure footed and feathery of landing, with Peter close up and light on the gray's shoulders.

"He jumps better'n some of them horses they got down around Templeton," one of the farm hands had said that spring when Peter was twelve and the Gray Boy over three. "You'd ought to take him down to the show they put on there in July," and Peter said nothing.

But he remembered the remark, and the next time he went to town for supplies he spied the poster of the horse show in the store window, and stood pondering it for several minutes. Templeton was becoming a summer resort for the riding crowd from the city. They were buying up old farms, bringing their horses with them because the country was so perfect, the road soft dirt, the weather not too hot. Beautiful horses they were too. Peter had seen them sometimes, tall and rangy hunters, sleek-coated and long-necked, their manes clipped short, bits and chains gleaming. Wonderful saddles they were, flat and broad, dull-polished, not much like the one he had, an old army saddle, although that didn't matter really. He had the Gray Boy and that was enough.

But there were money prizes, the poster said, twenty-five and even fifty dollars for some of the events—and the price of milk had dropped another cent recently. Peter had seen the smile fade from Mary Callender's face when she had opened that notice. He had understood when she had told him there could be no new saddle that summer.

The thought of appearing before a crowd of strangers, a huge crowd to him, was terrifying as he rode slowly homeward, but then he remembered that he would not be all alone, that the Gray Boy would be there too. And if somehow they should manage together to take home twenty-five or fifty dollars, sums almost beyond his comprehension, it would help Mary. And she would be proud of them. That thought was enough to make him forget his fear.

Days before the show, he had made his plans. He was, he told Mary, going to take an all-day ride, back into the hills with his rifle, looking for small game. He might not even be back for chores if—he looked at her questioningly—if that were all right. And Mary Callender, smiling quietly, said that it would be all right.

<hr />

And so at four o'clock on the morning of the big day, young Peter was in the barn, grooming and brushing the Gray Boy until the dappled coat shone, trying vainly to polish the stained snaffle bit, soaping the cracked reins and the scarred saddle. By six-thirty, the sun's warmth just beginning to be felt, they were off by the back road to the show grounds at Templeton, ten miles away.

The events were to begin at ten, the poster had said, but Peter waited over an hour, the Gray Boy cropping grass in the shade, before anyone appeared around the white-fenced show ring. Then, at last, a shiny yellow rig, red-wheeled, drove up and two men got down. One of them tall and very tanned, in breeches that flared above boots that gleamed brightly, came over toward him leisurely.

"Good morning," he greeted Peter, his smile friendly, welcoming. "You're early, aren't you?" and Peter nodded.

"I wanted time to rest my horse before—before the show started," he said gravely, and the tall man's eyes shifted to the horse, went over him appraisingly, lighting suddenly with interest.

"That's a beautiful horse," he said. "Is he yours?" And again Peter nodded.

"He's part Arabian," he said proudly, "and part Thoroughbred. I—we want to be in the show, he and I do. If we can," hopefully.

The tall man considered this gravely. "I don't know," he said at last. "This show's for hunters. Is your horse a hunter?"

"Oh, yes," Peter told him eagerly. "I hunt with him. Foxes sometime, and rabbits. I can shoot from his back and he won't move. He can follow game, too, almost like a dog, if I just guide him with my knees."

The tall man's eyes twinkled. "I see," he said. "Foxes, and sometimes rabbits, I believe you mentioned. Well, that's what we're supposed to hunt. In a little different manner, perhaps, but I guess it's all the same. Probably your way was first, at that.

What classes do you want to enter?" his eyes taking in the overalls, the stubby, square-toed boots, the faded blue shirt.

"I-I don't know," Peter stammered. "I—" but the tall man broke in.

"I'll tell you," he said quickly, understandingly. "You just leave all that to me. I'll be sort of your manager, if that's all right with you. But—" anxiously—"your horse can jump, can't he?"

"Oh, yes," Peter assured him.

Still the tall man hesitated; then, "You wouldn't mind showing me, would you? Just once around before the crowd gets here. So that—so that I'd know better where to enter you." And Peter nodded willingly, throwing the reins up over the Gray Boy's head, guiding him into the enclosure.

It was a strange place, new and with unfamiliar smells for the young horse, but Peter was on his back, reassuring him, and the jumps ahead were only jumps even if they were odd shaped, queer looking. Jumps were fun, and they took the first log hurdle easily, then the stone wall and finally the brush, cantering back to the tall man who watched them, smiling quietly.

"That was fine," he told young Peter, his voice relieved. "Now come over here and give me your name and I'll give you a badge." And Peter watched him fill out the blank, wondering vaguely why he wrote "Paid" in the space that said "Entry Fee," but forgetting that in the pride of the badge, large and white, with red lettering that spelled "Competitor." Not quite so large, perhaps, as the one his tall friend was wearing and that said "Chairman," but a very fine badge nevertheless.

"We'll enter you in the novice-hunter and the touch-and-out classes," his new friend said. "Now you go over there and watch things from the shade till I come for you." And Peter led the

Gray Boy back, not quite so nervous now, until the crowds began to arrive.

It was only a small show really, local and informal, but to small Peter it was terrifyingly grand, magnificent, with the perfectly dressed men and women arriving, laughing and casual, in their varnished carriages, their spanking teams. Some of them, a few, stopped for a second to look at the gray horse under the maple tree, but most of the onlookers were occupied with the big hunters being led about by grooms or by their owners, sleek, sinewy animals with their wonderful trappings, showy and expensive.

There was one person, though, who seemed to care more for the gray horse than for all the others, a small, persistent shadow of which young Peter was most acutely if not obviously aware. So much aware that finally, from a safe haven under the Gray Boy's shoulder, he stole a quick glance, and then, in spite of himself, another. She was a little girl, younger, Peter was quite sure, than himself even, a little girl with long golden curls in ringlets to her waist almost, and a miraculous, minute riding habit cut and swirled just like the older women's, and black riding boots, tiny and highly polished. A very perfect little horsewoman.

He busied himself needlessly with the Gray Boy's bridle, until at last a high and tinkling voice, a very respectful voice, inquired, "Is he—is he yours?" And Peter nodded shortly, the bridle requiring extra attention.

"He's a very lovely horse, isn't he?" the voice continued. "What's his name?"

"Gray Boy," Peter informed his small questioner from over his shoulder.

Still the voice persisted. "And—and are you going to ride him in the show?"

"Sure I am," Peter apprised her loftily. "We're in two—two classes."

Slowly and reluctantly, the small shadow drew away until Peter could safely steal another glance. They were very wonderful, those boots and that divided skirt. The curls were nice, but kind of silly.

Then, finally the events started and Peter climbed on the Gray Boy's back to see better, his heart pounding louder and louder, his hands moist as the time approached when he must go out before all that throng sitting in the rough stands and in their carriages drawn up around the ringside. He wanted terribly to ease the Gray Boy away and back into the familiar hills. But he didn't. He stayed, thinking of Mary Callender and that he couldn't run away.

And, at last, his tall friend sought him out. "All right, Peter," he smiled reassuringly, "you're next. Just hang this number over your shoulders and don't be frightened. You'll be all right," leading the way over to the ring entrance.

He was too intent, Peter was, his eyes too blurred, to notice the smiles that came his way, the rustled murmur that swept the onlookers as his turn came and the Gray Boy headed into the ring. He didn't realize, then, that they were with him, all the crowd, with the small boy in the faded overalls, the old-fashioned saddle and the beautiful horse. All he thought of was quieting the Gray Boy, who was panicky almost, but head up, tail flowing, ears pricked.

And then they were at the first jump, taking it cleanly, with the horse well in hand, over the second and the third, and then the turn.

That was where it happened, at the turn, just as they swung for the fourth jump. Someone cranked a car, a shiny red automobile, and the Gray Boy did not know about automobiles. They were new, the sudden roar terrifying, and he reared, swinging sideways at the jump, throwing small Peter to the ground, into the thick dust of the ring.

Then there were people running to him, to Peter, but he got up himself, dazed, bewildered, but unhurt, looking quickly for his horse, his horse that had failed him for the first time. And he saw the Gray Boy run across the ring and then stop, quivering and uncertain, back hunched, legs gathered, not knowing where to turn. And Peter whistled to him, making his lips pucker, forcing the familiar sound, and the Gray Boy heard and wheeled around, back to his small master, back to safety, trotting head up, nostrils wide, to Peter's side.

And then the crowd roared and clapped, but Peter scarcely heard. The shame was too great as, the Gray Boy's bridle in his hands, he trudged slowly back to the entrance, his tall friend at his side.

"It's all right, boy," the tall man was saying. "Don't feel too badly. It was his first time in a ring, probably his first automobile too. You come along and have some lunch with me, and then, later on, you'll have another chance to show them."

And Peter followed him, with only one large and unbidden tear furrowing the dust beneath his eyes, followed him over to a coach-and-four where there were other people, friendly and sympathetic, who fed him sandwiches and lemonade, bolstered his courage with kind words, watched smilingly as he excused himself to give the Gray Boy the oats that he had brought in the knotted sack.

The Gray Boy nuzzled his shoulder there in the shade of the maples, and small Peter stayed beside him, talking to him, until again the tall man sought them out.

"All ready once more, Peter," he smiled. "This time you'll show them. It's an old story for you now, and for the Gray Boy. This is the touch-and-out class, the big event. All you have to do is keep him jumping until you hit a bar. When you hit a bar, you're through. But you won't hit any."

And it wasn't bad this time: he knew people now, they were friendly. Even the Gray Boy seemed to sense that, to be eager to atone for his fault. This time they went around all seven jumps, not ticking one, landing cleanly, cantering back to the judges. But another horse made perfect score too, and they were off again, this time the bars raised higher. And still the Gray Boy jumped in hand, loving it now, whistling the breath through his nostrils.

But once more the other horse, the bay, went around in order, the crowd roaring. For the third time they took the ring, the bars up now so that the Gray Boy grunted as he cleared, but clearing every one. And this time the bay horse faltered at the second bar, crashing it to the ground, his rider swinging him away, disconsolate, but waving at small Peter.

That would be all, Peter thought, *he could go now;* but the tall man took his arm. "You've won it, Peter," he said jubilantly. "As nice a bit of riding as I've ever seen. You're fine, boy"—hugging his shoulder—"and now lead your horse out into the ring and get your prize."

There were people standing up in their carriages, in the stands, as Peter led the Gray Boy out, clapping and roaring their applause, with someone pinning a blue ribbon on the Gray Boy's bridle, and giving Peter an envelope that crackled in his hand. *That,* he thought, *must be the money,* and he wanted to open it right then and there, but didn't, stuffing it into a pocket of his overalls, leading the Gray Boy out, smiling through the dust that caked his face.

———◦———

At the gate he caught a quick glance, awe-inspiring and admiring, from the little girl in the riding habit, the little girl with the long golden curls, and his shoulders straightened back a shade farther, unconsciously, almost imperceptibly.

And then people crowded around, smiling, laughing, saying nice things, until finally small Peter said, "I—I'll have to be getting home now," and turned the Gray Boy back toward the hills and Mary Callender. It was not until he was two miles away that he dared open the envelope, and there were five ten dollar bills in it.

———◦———

That, big Peter Carlin thought now, guiding his car along the cement ribbon of road, *had been the proudest moment, almost, of his life. That moment when he had come into the dooryard and Mary Callender had come out from the kitchen door, seeing the blue ribbon on the Gray Boy's bridle as the horse stretched his head toward her.*

———◦———

"Why, Peter," she said, "why—what—" and he handed her the envelope, wrinkled and dirty, from his pocket.

"I—we brought you this, the Gray Boy and I," he said, getting down quickly and starting toward the watering trough, not looking back, too proud to have her see.

But she had run after him, Mary Callender had, gathering him in her arms, her voice strangely choked, holding him close, and saying only, "Oh, Peter, I'm so proud, so proud of you," until he had freed himself and gone marching off with the Gray Boy, to spend an hour sponging him, bedding him with fresh straw, talking gruffly to him, an arm over his neck.

The blue ribbon had been tacked beside the Gray Boy's stall, because, Peter said, it was *his* ribbon. He had won it, and people came from all over the countryside to admire and to be told about it. Peter never tired of having them come, in the week that followed; was glad to have them come—although he would not, of course, admit it.

Glad until that morning when the red automobile drove into the yard, the first car almost that had ever been on the farm, and a man had gotten out stiffly, because ten miles was quite a drive in those days. A man who was not Peter's tall friend from the show, as he noted disappointedly, but who was nice looking and who had a girl with him. A little girl, smaller than Peter, with long golden curls and, today, a crisp ironed dress that flared straight out above bare legs, tanned and scratched here and there. The same little girl who had stood beside him, beside Peter, there outside the show ring.

The two hired men, Jake and Martin, had come out to gape at the car, and Mary Callender walked down to greet the visitors, with Peter following at a distance, trying to appear disinterested, as if such things as cars and little girls with blond curls were far beneath him. But drawn nevertheless.

"Good morning"—the tall man had bowed to Mary—"my name is Holden, and this is my little daughter Sally. She, and I, too, wanted to come out and see the gray horse that your boy had at the Templeton show. This is the place, isn't it?"

And Mary Callender smiled. "Yes," she said, "this is the place. Bring the Gray Boy out, will you, Peter, so that we can see him." And Peter had gone stiffly into the barn, pausing to run a quick brush over the gray horse, and then had led him out into the sunlight.

They stood back, the two visitors, admiringly, with Peter very busy at the halter rope and pretending that the Gray Boy was hard to hold, while Mary told about raising the horse and how Peter had trained it.

"He's a beautiful animal," the tall man said finally. "I don't suppose"—glancing quickly at Peter and then at Mary Callender—"that you would ever want to sell him?" And Peter's eyes shot to Mary's face, startled, struck with terror at the sudden overwhelming thought, but quickly reassured as Mary shook her head.,

"Oh, no," she smiled quietly, "we'd never sell the Gray Boy, would we, Peter? You see, he's Peter's horse, not mine," and the tall man nodded understandingly.

"I thought that would be the case," he said, "but Sally here was so taken with the horse that she's been after me ever since the show. She rides quite well herself and I'm looking for something for her. But I can understand," and Peter led the Gray Boy back to the stable, hastily, fearfully, lest only by looking they take his horse away.

He stayed there beside the Gray Boy in the stall until he heard the red car roar away, and then he went up to the house, filling the wood box silently, wanting to speak but not quite bringing himself to it, until Mary, busy at the stove, said, "Imagine their thinking we would ever let the Gray Boy go! Why, I'd almost sooner have you go away yourself, Peter," and then the weight was lifted and he could smile again.

"He's no horse for a girl, anyway," he said scornfully. "He's a man's horse," and he went on out and down to the barn, whistling cheerfully.

Jake and Martin were working in the cow stable, and he could hear them talking as he approached silently over the hay-strewn floor, stopping suddenly as his mind grasped their words.

"Five hundred dollars," Jake was saying. "That's what he said he'd pay if they ever did want to sell. Said the Gray Boy was worth that much. Five hundred dollars for a horse—an' a saddle horse at that! What five hundred dollars wouldn't do on this farm right now, what with the price of milk droppin' another cent this mornin'. I don't see how Mary'll get through the winter, what with grain goin' up an' all. Have to sell some stock, I reckon."

"Better to sell the horse," Martin opined. "Cows is business—a horse like that's an extravagance."

"She won't never sell the horse," Jake declared, "not with Peter so crazy over him," and Peter turned, tiptoeing out of the barn and down the wood lane, sudden, sinking fear gripping at his heart, panicking him, paralyzing his thoughts.

Five hundred dollars. But he couldn't let the Gray Boy go. He couldn't. Never. He'd rather die, much rather. But five hundred dollars. He tried to think. Money he had never known much about. He never had any himself—never needed it. And Mary couldn't really need it either. Not with all this land, all the farm and the stock. It wasn't possible, he tried to tell himself. Jake and Martin must be wrong. They were mistaken. That was it—they just didn't know.

But still the fear lay heavy, crowding out all else.

<hr />

That evening after supper he sat beneath the oil lamp, thumbing the pages of the mail-order catalogue, not seeing even the pictures of the saddles, the bridles, that fascinated him ordinarily, while Mary, glasses on, worked over papers at her desk in the corner. Finally, he spoke.

"I betcha," he said, grammar forgotten, "I betcha that grain for all our stock costs an awful lot every winter. I betcha it costs even pretty near fifty dollars, just for grain." Waiting expectantly, hopefully, as Mary turned, smiling wearily, glasses pushed up on her forehead.

"I wish it *did* cost fifty dollars, Peter," she said, "but nearer ten times that, I'm afraid, much nearer."

And he stared at her wide-eyed, uncomprehending. Five hundred dollars just for grain! But, with one faint hope, "Humph," he said disdainfully, "but I betcha we get more than that every week just for our milk, don't we?" And again Mary Callender smiled, her face tired.

"Well, no, Peter, not quite that. Not in a whole summer with prices what they are. But"—cheerfully—"we'll get along. We always have," turning back to her papers, while Peter sat, sensing, somehow, the droop to the straight shoulders in the gingham dress. Five hundred dollars.

<hr />

For two days he had wrestled with his problem, lying awake at night in his room over the kitchen, working mechanically, automatically, in the field, and then, on the third day, he had made up his mind.

Mary was away that day, visiting, and at nine o'clock young Peter led the Gray Boy out, cleaning him carefully, saddling him without a word, and heading toward the Holden estate, eight miles away. He went through the woods and across fields for one last jump over brooks and stone walls, his face expressionless, stolid, all the way and right up to the broad lawn and pillared house where the Holdens lived.

Mr. Holden was in a deep chair on the piazza, and he got up as

Sally came eagerly through the door. Peter halted the Gray Boy at the steps.

"I've brought you my horse," he said simply. "May I have the money, please?"

And Sally cried delightedly as her father, taken aback, stammered, "Why-why—" in quick succession. "Yes, of course," he said quietly, "I'll get it for you right away," vanishing into the house as Peter stood at the Gray Boy's head, looking anywhere away from the girl, shaking his head at her eager questions.

"Could he single-foot?" "Did he shy ever?" "Did you have to tether him?" And finally, doubtfully, "But-but if you're very, very fond of him, Peter, I wouldn't want to take him from you."

That had broken him almost, those last words, shaken his firm resolution, but then, mercifully, the check was in his hands and he made himself speak. "He-he likes carrots," he said, "at night," and this time he did not look back.

"But don't you want the saddle and the bridle?" Mr. Holden called, and Peter only shook his head, running, almost, over the long velvety lawn and into the woods, stopping his ears as the Gray Boy whinnied shrilly.

———⇒◦⇐———

He could remember now, to this day, the spot a mile from the Holdens', the spot among the white birches where the grass was high and where he had lain with his face buried in the sod until the sun had set and the shadows were long. Then he had gone home. A person less wise, less fine and understanding than Mary Callender would have done the wrong thing when the boy came home that night. Would have cried over him and tried to make him take the Gray Boy back again. But Mary didn't. She knew that life for Peter would be hard and full of bitter disappointments, self-denials; and she realized, most importantly, why he had done what he had done. She only took his hand firmly, shaking it as if he were a man.

"You've helped me, Peter," she said quietly, "helped me out when I honestly didn't know which way to turn. And I appreciate it. You're my partner now, really."

And those words had done more to square the small shoulders, to lighten the empty misery in the boy's heart than anything else could have done. He had helped her and she understood.

But it wasn't that easy, all of it. He stuck it out for a week, young Peter did, and then he gave in. He had to see his horse. And so, one evening after chores, he slipped away, walking the eight miles across country to the Holden place, circling wide to the barn and finding, finally, the stall where the Gray Boy was waiting, ears pricked, feet pawing as he heard the familiar step. For two hours they were together there in the dark stall, and then the long walk home, alone for Peter, creaking up the back stairs to his room at last.

Every night, almost, for the next two weeks he made that trip, made it on foot after the long day's work, thinking that no one knew. But Mary Callender had known, but said nothing.

And then there came that time when he was so tired that he went to sleep in the thick straw beside the Gray Boy's head, sleeping soundly, exhaustedly, until the morning, when Mr. Holden, coming down to the barn for an early morning ride with his small daughter, found him there. He drove him home in the red automobile, and for half an hour he and Mary Callender talked in her little office room. Then they called Peter.

"Peter," said Mr. Holden, "we've been wondering what to do with the Gray Boy in the winter, for the eight months that we are not up here. We can't very well keep him in the city, and we wondered, Sally and I, if you would mind taking care of him for us. Just to help us out."

And Peter nodded dumbly, too thankful for words, too overjoyed.

And so the Gray Boy had come back, back for a part of the time at least, the greater part. And it had meant, he told himself now, big Peter Carlin did, driving along alone, that life had been full for him throughout the years that followed. Full and very happy, really, with new things, the state college, new friends, but always the old things that were best and closest to his heart and would be always.

It had been hard, in that first year after college, to leave the hill country, to leave the Gray Boy and to leave Mary Callender. But she had urged it for him.

"I want you to go, Peter," she had said. "You must. There's— there's nothing in a hill farm anymore, nothing but a home for you to come back to when you can. It will make me prouder of you, Peter, prouder almost than anything else ever could, to see you going ahead, doing the things that you are fit to do. And," she added, smiling, "I'll be here, Peter, here where I belong, for many years, I hope. And you'll come back often, Peter. Please."

And he *had* come back, back from the work found through the kindly offered help of Mr. Holden; back, as the years went by, and not so many years, to ride the old familiar trails again. Not so fast or so far as in the days when the Gray Boy had been younger, not so gallantly perhaps, but with the same quiet pleasure, the gray horse still striving to be keen, head up, ears pricked for Peter's voice.

Sometimes on those rides, there had been little Sally Holden beside him. Sometimes really there herself, astride another horse, but not often, because he would not let himself ask her for that. It wasn't, he had told himself, the thing for him to do, to see her often. It wasn't fair to her. He had his life, his way to make, and she had hers already made.

But always through the years and at his work, successful now, there was her image in his mind—the image, crystal clear and lasting, of the little girl at Templeton, the little girl of golden curls and the miraculous riding habit. An image changing now as she had changed, to one that laughed and was merry—slender, lithe, her eyes a lighter blue almost, her hair more golden. Those thoughts he put away as best he could.

The Gray Boy was at home now always, at home on the hill farm, his days of work that had been fun all over, past. Only a few short months it had been, that Peter Carlin had gone down to see him, down through the shadowy barns and to the box stall bedded soft, knee deep in straw, where the Gray Boy stood. Feeble and stiff he was now, coat rough, eyes failing, but ears still alert for the familiar footsteps, soft muzzle stretching over the low barrier.

And they had stood there silently, tall Peter Carlin and Mary Callender, his hand through the stringy mane, and then he turned away. "I hate to see him that way," he had said, his voice low. "I want to think of him always alive and keen and eager, the way—the way he was that day at Templeton. The day he won his blue ribbon."

And Mary Callender had said, "I know," softly, "I know. But he isn't suffering, Peter. It isn't that. I wouldn't let that happen. He's only old. Some morning he—he just won't get up, that's all."

"I hope I'll be here then," he had said. "You'll let me know, won't you?"

But he had not been there on that morning. This morning now, this dull gray day. At six o'clock he had received the telegram, just five words, nothing more—"He didn't get up, Peter"—and signed "Mary." And he had dressed to make this drive alone.

He was almost there now, through Templeton and up the long, familiar hill, the maples bare, leaves swirling on the ground, the gray-shingled house straw-packed for the winter, the barns below, with Mary, in the same old long tweed coat, coming out the door of the horse cell.

"Is he—" Peter forced the words, and she shook her head, her smile gentle and strong, but very tender, understanding.

"Not yet, Peter, not yet."

And then he was there, tall Peter Carlin, on his knees in the thick straw, head down to that old gray one, tired and heavy, worn-out now. And Mary Callender turned away to let them have what was theirs and could be only theirs.

And as she turned, half groping, a car had topped the hill, coming fast, then swinging to a stop, with Sally, little Sally Holden, hesitating, not quite sure.

"I heard," she said, "I heard and *had* to come. Do you suppose—oh, Mary, do you think he'll mind if I—"

And Mary Callender's smile was quiet, but almost happy now, contented, as she said, "No, Sally, he won't mind, I think," standing aside to let the girl go through, the big door closing slowly.

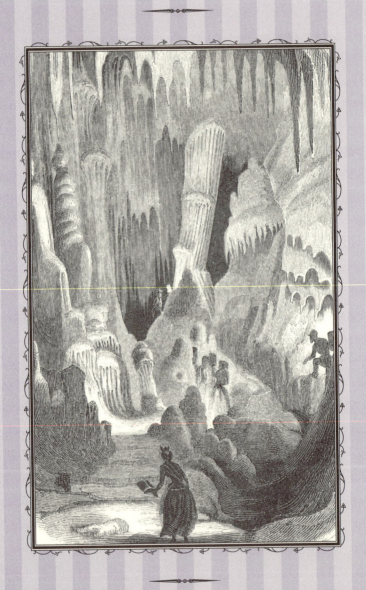

WHATH YO NAME?

Carolyn Rathbun-Sutton

*W*here friendships are concerned, most of us are very selective; far be it from us to choose someone unworthy of such a gift. And people with disabilities would be the very last to merit such inclusion. Wouldn't they?

t's going to be one of those hot sun-'n'-lizard days, I mused to myself, *but I'll stay cool down in the cave.*

Tucking in a stray end of my blouse, I glanced at my colorful guide uniform reflecting in the Moaning Cavern gift shop window.

I had never had such a delightful summer job: giving tours at this natural wonder and popular tourist attraction near Vallecito, California. Opening the door to the gift shop, I stepped in.

"Guess what, Carolyn," Deena greeted me, "your first tour this morning is a group of twenty-five mentally retarded adults on their way home from a week of camping. Good luck!"

I stopped in the doorway. "What? Wait a minute!" I said, but she hurried into the darkroom to develop a set of tour group photos.

It's not that I was prejudiced against mentally handicapped people, you understand. It's just that they are so strange and unpredictable to be around. In fact, the expression *mentally retarded* always reminded me of the time I walked through a psychiatric ward with my hospital administrator father and heard a patient screaming from her padded cell. The memory made me shudder.

OK, I told myself. *Let's think this through.* So far this summer, without too much stress, I had managed claustrophobic tourists, boisterous Boy Scout troops, and even a few squalling babies. But how would I ever get twenty-five uncoordinated, possibly dangerous, mentally handicapped adults down and then *back up* 236 steps on the cavern's see-through metal staircase?

I was getting scared. While I waited for the group to arrive, I dusted around the cash register and rearranged merchandise on the gift shop shelves.

All too soon their white tour bus wound its way down the

narrow road and into the gravel parking lot. Stepping out onto the porch, I surveyed the situation. The driver backed out of the door at the front of the bus.

I'll bet he doesn't dare turn his back on them, I thought nervously. *And I'm supposed to lead them down the staircase? Ha! I just hope no one is carrying a knife!*

"Now listen, everyone," the driver called from the bus's front door, "just keep your seats! Stay exactly where you are while I go buy the tickets."

I noticed several of the passengers, necks craned about, staring out the windows at me. Feeling mild revulsion, I avoided their gaze and forced a smile at the driver coming up the steps.

"Well, we made it!" he beamed. "Where do I get the tickets?" I pointed to the gift shop.

Soon he emerged and returned to the bus.

"All right, everyone, let's go see a cave!" he called jovially. The passengers, some of them struggling, rose from their seats and jostled into the aisle of the bus.

Here we go, I thought as they came off the bus, assisted by several chaperons. How perfectly they fitted my stereotyped mental image of what retarded people look like. Some walked with abrupt, twitching movements; others looked about them with vacant stares; one man was drooling; and a partially blind man in his twenties, lightly rocking his head back and forth, clung to the arm of a male chaperon.

I couldn't help feeling sorry for the group's escorts, locked into a demanding—even repulsive—responsibility like this. One of the chaperons, a gray-haired woman in her late fifties, smiled at me. Sympathetically I returned her smile, thinking how hard it must be to keep up a pleasant front in her position. How embarrassed she must feel, having to always be with this group of people!

Into the gift shop they came, smelling like the smoke from a week's worth of campfires. I tried not to breathe.

"This way, please," I announced, ushering them into the room housing the cave's original vertical drop, enclosed by a protective fence.

I hope no one tries to jump the fence!

"So glad you could all come out to the cave today." I smiled mechanically, feeling a twinge of guilt at my lie. "This is the cave's original entrance," I began my lecture, trying not to look at the man who was still drooling or at the young woman with mongoloid features who stood uncomfortably close to me.

During the first part of the presentation, I found myself focusing more and more on the faces of the chaperons, most of whom were middle-aged or elderly. I detected nothing except peaceful expressions, even when they were bumped by their constantly moving charges.

"Are there any questions?" I paused, silently planning my strategy to get this group down the spiral staircase.

"Yeth, I hab a question," lisped a slightly built Hispanic man with thick glasses. Then he stopped and looked about with uncertainty.

"That's fine, Danny," the tall, graying bus driver reassured him. "Ask your question."

An eager grin spread across Danny's face as he again focused on me.

"Whath yo name?" he asked.

Smiling indulgently, I sighed. "My name is Carolyn. Now we are going to continue our tour down into the cave." Two women in the group who understood what I said, giggled with childlike excitement.

Cautiously we made our way down to the upper platform in Moaning Cavern's Big Room, then down the spiral staircase.

I noticed how carefully, compassionately, the chaperons shepherded their motley group: encouraging clumsy Hilda, complimenting Bob on how well he was moving his legs, thanking Nancy for not complaining on the long trip down. Funny, but I had never thought of this handicapped group as individual personalities who answered to their own names.

Although I no longer felt physically threatened by these visitors, I still found them unappealing. Again, I wondered about the patience of their escorts. Why would a person in his right mind give up life's normal adventures, slowing down to a little child's pace—intellectually as well as physically—in order to care for people such as these? It was beyond my understanding.

At the bottom of Moaning Cavern's Big Room, an expanse large enough to contain the Statue of Liberty, I launched into the last part of my lecture. I pointed out the thirty-five-foot Igloo, the suspended Angel Wings, the MGM Lion, and other distinctive formations found in that roomy arena.

Although I had been here dozens of times, the serenity and grandeur of the highly decorated cave chamber never failed to overpower me and dwarf me as I looked into what resembled a vast crystal cathedral. It was with a twinge of reluctance that I brought every tour to an end.

"Are there any questions before we go back up the staircase?" I asked one final time.

"What's your name?" asked a stringy-haired, oversized woman in a flower-print dress. Where had I heard that question before?

"It's Carolyn," I answered, and a sponsor winked at me good-naturedly. "Any other questions? Yes, Danny."

"Whath yo name?" he asked, as he had at the beginning of the lecture.

"Danny," I answered, "you know what my name is. It's Carolyn." He smiled and nodded.

Just then the tall, nearly blind man, who had been clinging to his chaperon's arm ever since he'd entered the cave, released his hold and awkwardly pushed his way between Danny and the drooler. Walking unsteadily toward me, he stopped a few inches from my face. He leaned over, squinted into my eyes, and asked, "What's youw name?"

I could smell the outdoor aroma coming from his clothing. The entire group seemed taken aback and waited in silence for my answer.

I forced one last professional smile into my face and sighed, "Why, it's Carolyn."

He looked back at the others and gleefully repeated. "Why, it's Cawolyn." Then he added, "And she's nice."

Without warning, he suddenly turned toward me, threw his arms wide open, and gave me the biggest spontaneous bear hug I had had in a long time. Instinctively I returned his gesture with a quick squeeze. This unexpected encounter brought laughter from the group, and the drooler even applauded. I couldn't help laughing with them.

As the blind man's chaperon stepped forward and took his elbow, my prejudice against these gentle visitors evaporated.

"You're Carolyn," said the woman with mongoloid features, nodding approvingly during the trip back out of the cave. I returned her nod.

Both Bob and Nancy told me, "You're nice," when I assisted

them on a few steps. Hilda reached out and lightly touched me as I passed her puffing heavily on her way up the stairs. Others smiled or stared in a comfortable, unaffected manner.

Suddenly I realized, with a bit of a start, that these handicapped people had accepted *me* as one of them. An hour before, this realization would have disgusted or frightened me. But now, for the first time since beginning work that morning, I felt good—*very* good.

⚊⚊⚊◆⚊⚊⚊

Normally I said good-bye to my tour groups at the top of the cavern steps as we emerged into the gift shop. This time I found myself following them out the door and watching a bit wistfully as they boarded the bus.

Again I couldn't help noticing the courtesy with which the chaperons treated each individual as they saw the group members to their seats.

"You did very well in the cave!" announced the bus driver to the passengers, wiping his shiny forehead with a blue handkerchief. "Because you were so good," he continued with unflagging energy, "we are going to have a special picnic on the way home. How would you like that?"

Amid the group's approving chatter, he slid into the driver's seat, fastened his seat belt, and turned the key in the ignition.

Thoughtfully, I leaned over the railing of the front porch while the bus turned around on the dusty gravel. I watched the vehicle lurch several times, gaining momentum as it turned back toward the parking lot entrance.

I spotted Nancy's cherubic face, and the blind man aimlessly moved his head about.

"Good-bye! Good-bye!" several began yelling.

"Bye now," the bus driver cheerfully called from his window as he drove past.

"Bye," I answered, feeling a sting in my eyes. I could see Danny's frantic wave.

"You're nisth," he called out, chin lifted above his half-closed window.

"So are you, Danny," I managed through a tight throat. "So are you."

Carolyn Rathbun-Sutton

former editor of *The Junior Guide,* today lives and writes in a mountainous area not far from Grants Pass, Oregon. This story was featured in *Insight's Most Unforgettable Stories.*

THE GIRL AT THE
TELEPHONE

Author Unknown

In today's hectic society, more and more we deal with machines rather than people. It was not so in the early days of the telephone. The operator handled your call personally. The operator was a human being, a friend, who might—perish the thought!—break down.

ive me Greene, 2120, please."

The voice which came back was a trifle metallic, as if it had caught the quality from contact with the wire over which it traveled. "Line's busy; shall I call you?"

"If you will, please." Then with sudden curiosity, Constance added, "You're not our regular operator, are you? Your voice sounds so different."

The telephone girl's gasp of surprise was distinctly audible. She was not prepared for the question. Long usage had accustomed her to being regarded as a part of a mechanism, necessary to communication like the receiver or the connecting wire, but hardly more qualified than either to be regarded as a person. "No, I'm new here," she answered shortly. "Other girl broke down."

A few minutes later, Constance's bell jingled a preemptory summons. "You wanted Greene, 2120, didn't you? Here they are."

"Oh, thanks! By the way, what was the matter with the other girl?"

"Oh, most of us break down after a while!" said the telephone girl. "Just come down to one of the exchanges, and sit around for half an hour watching and listening, if you think this is anybody's easy job." And then she made the connection with Greene, 2120, and Constance was soon perfecting plans with her closest friend for a festive afternoon a little later in the week.

But the thought of the telephone girl who had broken down clung to her with strange persistence. She found herself wondering what sort of personality went with the pleasant voice which was so familiar. She imagined her a girl with a gentle face and rather wistful eyes. Constance fancied that she had never looked very strong. Sometimes there was a weariness in the voice, unmistakable in spite of its obliging promptness.

Constance had heard the voice of the telephone girl under all sorts of conditions. She had noticed it first because of its unfailing courtesy and sweetness, in all the ups and downs of telephonic communication. Callers, even considerate ones, find it hard not to blame the telephone operator when the number they are calling does not answer. Several times Constance had spoken with impatient protest, and at once felt rebuked by the disarming gentleness of the operator's answer. She grew to experience a sensation of mild pleasure in recognizing the familiar tones, a satisfaction too vague to make a deep impression, and yet unmistakable.

But the telephone girl had had a share in experiences more memorable. There was the day when Constance's mother fell, and lay in a senseless heap at the foot of the stairs, and Constance, running to the telephone almost beside herself with terror, had only been able to shriek, "Oh, tell the doctor to come quick! I'm afraid Mother's killed." To the end of her life she would never forget the brave voice which came back over the phone and steadied her nerves.

"Yes, I'll get him for you at once. But which doctor do you want? Yes, just the name. Never mind the number."

That long illness put the telephone girl to the test. Again and again there were imperative calls for the doctor, for Constance's father, for the drug store. She was not only patient and faithful, but there was sympathy in the tone in which she repeated the number. In those agonizing days, the sound of a stranger's voice at the other end of the wire would have jarred as much on Constance's nerves as suddenly having a stranger in the house.

And now she had broken down. Constance, remembering her

first and only visit to a large telephone exchange, did not wonder. As she had watched the nimble fingers at work, and heard the monotonous repetition of numbers, it had seemed to her that a week of such work would drive her crazy. And then she found herself met by an unreasonable regret. She could not help wishing that before the sweet-voiced operator had broken down, she had found an opportunity to express appreciation for her faithful service.

Twenty-four hours later, Constance had a conversation with the chief operator. "We can't give names," was the answer to her partially stated errand. "But if you have a complaint—"

"I only wished to inquire after her and to let her know that I appreciate her being so faithful and patient while we had sickness at the house."

"Oh!" said the chief operator, and her voice, too, betrayed astonishment. After that she talked less like a chief operator and more like a human being. She explained that No. 117—even in her sudden unbending she did not violate the rule which called for secrecy regarding the name of the operator—was only temporarily incapacitated, it was hoped. She expected to come back, and they were anxious to have her, as she was a girl whose place it would be rather difficult to fill.

"And if I want to send her a few flowers, it can be arranged, can't it?" Constance asked, and the chief operator explained how this would be possible. And when Constance hung up her receiver a quarter of a minute later, she was sure that never again could she use a telephone without realizing that there was a real person in back of the voice, which hitherto had seemed only a part of a wonderful nineteenth-century invention.

A day or two later, a pale girl who was trying to take a nap on a rickety couch in a third-floor bedroom, kept rousing herself to look at a cluster of pink roses, which stood on a small stand beside her—big, velvety blossoms, whose fragrance made the little room smell like a summer garden. And almost every time she looked, she took up a card lying on the stand, and read its inscription, while a little smile played about her lips:

"Phone West, 3710 sends sympathy to No. 117, with grateful remembrance of past kindness, and best wishes for a speedy recovery."

MY EYES WITH A WAGGIN' TAIL

Joseph Tolve Jr.

riends are . . . uh . . . people, aren't they? Well . . . what if you were blind—would you still feel that way (living as you do in total darkness)?

Certainly Mr. Tolve had his doubts.

arly in August I was sitting in the living room of Guiding Eyes for the Blind, waiting to learn the name of my new guide dog. Around me I could hear the nervous conversations of eleven others, waiting as anxiously as I. Some were grieving for a dog just departed; others were here for the first time. All of us had come on a most important mission to tiny and, I'm told, beautiful Yorktown Heights in Westchester County, New York.

After what seemed an endless wait, I was finally called in to meet John. He was the man who had trained the dog I was to receive and who would teach the two of us to walk together.

"His name is Rally," John said. "He's a Bouvier des Flandres, from a breed originally used in Belgium to herd cattle. Male. Twenty-seven inches tall. Weighs one hundred and eighty-seven pounds. Salt-and-pepper coloring." John, I was to discover, didn't like to waste words.

The following afternoon I sat alone in the middle of a room, waiting for my introduction. The piece of meat in my hand I would offer to the dog as his first and only bribe. I heard the shuffling of John's feet and Rally's paws on the wooden stairs outside and stirred uneasily. It was a critical moment.

John opened the door and said from across the room, "OK, Joe, relax. Let him have the meat and let him explore you, smell you. I'll hand you the leash. Take him to your room, pet him, but don't rush him. If he wants to be petted, he'll stay there next to you. If he doesn't, he'll lie on the floor at your feet. Don't force yourself on him."

The trainer approached me slowly and I could hear Rally sniffing the air. As they reached my side, I put out the hand containing meat. Rally checked it, took it, and chewed it. Finished, he smelled my ankle, then went up my leg on another sniffing expedition. John handed me the leash. "Here you are. Take it easy."

I moved carefully toward the doorway, remembering there was one step down to negotiate. It would be awful to trip the very first time I was with my new dog. Stepping off boldly, I paced down the hallway, counting the open doors with my extra sense. How much I had depended on the inner antenna of my precious sixth sense since losing my sight nearly nine years before. Now, walking beside me was a four-legged fellow who, if all went well, would be much more than a mere antenna.

In my room I petted Rally for a moment, but he tired of it quickly and lay down at my feet.

Four o'clock. A knock sounded and I heard John say, "Rally's dish is to the left of the door, Joe. Feed him, and give him water in the basin under the bathroom sink."

Hooking Rally's collar to the bed chain, I crossed the room to get his food. As I put it in front of him I felt a tingle of excitement at his eagerness. That he wanted to eat was a sign things were going well. Pressing both feet to the sides of the pan, I tried to hold his dinner in place as he ate, but his tongue was stabbing so hard at the light aluminum, it was impossible to keep the container in one spot. Finally the eating sounds stopped and I checked the pan. Finished, and so quickly. Glowing with the certainty he felt comfortable with me, I put his leash on and took him into the bathroom for his water. He gulped nearly the whole pan, another good sign.

That evening Rally and I went to the dining room where I was to keep him under the table and prone at my side. The dogs had been trained together and very much wanted to have a reunion, so it was a busy meal. After dinner I went to my room with Rally at heel, put him on his bed chain, undressed and got into bed. But not to sleep.

I was hardly under the covers when the dog began to cry. No ordinary crier, this one had been orchestrated, and he put it all together for my first night's entertainment. His cry became a screech and the screech became a howl and when I snapped, "No! No, Rally!" nothing changed.

There was an emergency button over my bed and after repeated efforts only raised his decibel level, I rang. The trainer was at the door almost instantly. "John," I started, "he's been crying very . . ."

"I know. Heard him upstairs." By his voice I knew he was standing near Rally, and I felt the dog tugging furiously at the bedpost, trying to get John to take him from my room.

"No! Down!" John stamped his foot and turned to me. "If he starts this again, sound off so he knows who's boss and he'll lie down."

A minute after the trainer left the room, Rally was at it again, and again I couldn't quiet him. When I had to call for help a third time, it was in desperation. I was being rejected.

"Now, here's Rally's leash, Joe." John's words were gentle. "If he starts to cry like that once more, hit it against your bed as hard as you can and yell, 'NO!'"

For angry hours I lay listening to the off-key whimpering of my one-man band. I had had to use the leash on the bed five or six times just to get his crying down to that level. Now, cheek pressed against the pillow, I began to smolder. It wasn't fair that I should get this Bouvier-something-or-other with hair so long it covered his eyes. He was shabby all over and I was jealous of the others getting handsome, smooth golden retrievers. What had they told me this breed used to do in Belgium? Herd cattle? That's where he belonged!

"No! Stop it!" I wildly flailed the leash at my bedsheet and this time the whimpering stopped. My nose burned and tears wet my pillowcase. I was sure it was I who had failed to make our relationship a success.

In the morning we were bused to Peekskill where we would do most of our training, since Yorktown Heights has no sidewalks. Neither Rally nor I had had much to say to each other after such a miserable night and I took a backseat in the bus. I wanted the others to go first, fearing what might happen when it finally came my turn to disembark.

"We're going to walk a one-block area today," John told us. "We will make only right turns. When your dog stops at the curb, move your right foot back, extend your right hand and motion to the right, saying the name of your dog and 'Right!'"

The air through the opened window was August warm and my collar was already wet with perspiration. Nervous, I lectured myself for my fears.

"OK, Joe," came the trainer's call. It was Rally's and my turn, but I moved slowly down the aisle of the bus. I could hear the excitement outside; the others praising their dogs for their performance. What if I blundered just getting off the bus? My heart pounded furiously.

"Rally, come!"

He executed perfectly, and it was almost impossible to contain the emotion welling in my throat when I stopped and he moved promptly to the heel position at my left. Only time for a quick pat and a breathless, "Good boy."

"Put the leash over your left wrist now." John's tone was reassuring. He must understand. "Have the two straps flat on the palm of your hand so you can take his harness and still have the leash ready, if Rally makes a mistake. We're not going to worry the dog about side bushes or overhead obstacles today. We're only asking him for right turns. All right, take his harness and give him the command, 'Forward!'"

I dropped my hand to Rally's harness and felt the power under it. As I gave the command I stepped out and was immediately glad I had, for he charged ahead with a great surge of power. I found myself flying down the sidewalk, walking faster than I had ever walked since losing my sight, and I was a fast cane walker.

We got to the first curb and Rally put on the brakes. Stopped on a dime! Fortunately I had been keeping my full attention on the movement of the harness. No time for discipline, even if he had nearly sent me into orbit. It didn't matter; Rally was beginning to like me.

"Rally, right!"

Again he obeyed the command with such enthusiastic precision that his one hundred and fifty-plus pounds nearly took me off my feet as he cut across my front from the left.

"Keep up with him, Joe!" shouted John from behind and Rally stopped abruptly to turn toward John. He had to see his trainer, his real friend and the man he had come to love during seven months of training.

I could hear John's slow approach and now Rally was tugging to meet him. "No!" The crack of leather in John's hand shattered the rapport, and Rally got the message. My heart went out to both of them. *How hard it must be,* I thought, *for these men to make the dogs they have trained and loved actually dislike them. But it was necessary, if this shaggy coated, happy-go-lucky bundle of power was to become my eyes.*

"Stay with him, Joe!" John's voice was tense as I moved out

again. "He's a fast mover; keep with him! Don't hold back against that harness; move with him!"

I found myself running down the sidewalk, the wind whistling past my ears. Fears were forgotten. I was free. Free at last! I had a dog who wanted to walk fast as I did, a dog who wanted to move out and explore the world.

That night we two huddled together in my room and talked about our day. I fondled his pointed ears and felt his short tail wag slowly, almost sadly. I knew I was starting to love Rally. He was such a loyal type. Why had I been surprised that he hated to give up John? Such a confused fellow he must be tonight. I stroked the hair that grew over his eyes. Even that seemed suddenly beautiful.

Two weeks later we were released to go home. That afternoon the two of us had passed our subway test in Manhattan and were pronounced fit and ready for anything in the world. We'd found our way through the crowds to the change-making booth, passed through the turnstile and waited calmly through the clatter and shriek of the arriving subway train. Without a hitch we'd made our trip and brought ourselves back again and, to tell the truth, we were really quite smug about it.

We became so close in the years that followed. Could it really have been only two? There was something so grand, so beautiful about my dog, and perhaps the grandest, most beautiful thing about him was the way he made himself an extension of me. Rally's eyes were my eyes. My moods and needs became his moods and needs. If I was downcast, his tail dragged and his taut muscles seemed limp. If I was exhilarated, there was no restraining his own joy. We were ready together now to make a productive contribution to life.

Our first real effort must have been especially rugged for Rally:

I took a job as a masseur in the YMCA in Port Chester, next to my hometown. It called for long hours, and every day Rally was with me at the side of the massage table in the men's locker room. Not far from my work area was a sauna, and no one can imagine the temperature in our low-ceilinged room. I thought of poor Rally in all that heat. He was trim now and didn't have that long coat, but still . . . he was great. Greater than I had ever imagined a dog could be. Patient beyond human endurance, he lay in harness all day long without a single complaint.

One day when business was slack, I took Rally with me to the pool area to wait while I took a dip. I marched him past the life-guard and the people talking at the side of the pool, and left him at the end where there was no chance of his being underfoot. With only the usual, "Stay!" I walked to the edge, dove in and started swimming to the opposite end fifty yards away.

All of a sudden there was a squawk that sounded like a human cry of consternation and I heard a huge splash behind me. A roar of delight went up on all sides and I knew immediately who had followed me into the pool—a dog who loved me so much that even though he didn't know what swimming was all about, he wanted to be sure I was all right. My heart swelled with the joy I felt to have such a friend.

He must have thought *I told you so* the time I deserted him for the tandem bicycle. A metal drain grille in a parking lot gave way and two cyclists went flying. During the ride in the ambulance poor Rally sat beside the stretcher, his nose wet and warm with worry as it pressed against my arm. Without a word, he was say-ing everything that could be said.

My father brought me a message three days later. "Rally's not eating, Joe. He's not going outside. He just sits in your room all day at the foot of your bed." Somehow arrangements were made to have Rally allowed in a private hospital. He began eating again, and was happy we could be together all day.

Five weeks later I was in physical therapy, training to walk with a brace that went from hip to heel. After leaning on a nurse's arm for a few days, I was ready to make a test run with my buddy. I was amazed at his wisdom, for though he had always been such a fast walker, now he moved slowly and gently, pacing himself exactly to my step.

In the year that followed with that brace, Rally and I were out almost every day, walking to strengthen my leg. During the winter I saw a most remarkable demonstration of my dog's intelligence whenever I started to slip on ice or snow. If I was going forward, he would backpedal with incredible speed to keep me upright. If I started to fall backward, he would jerk forward on his harness just enough to keep me on my feet. He had a phenomenal batting average of success.

It was a great opportunity when I got the chance to take training as an X-ray developer. For four weeks we commuted to New Rochelle and I loved the work. My teachers were so patient in showing me how to process the film. The only one with more patience was Rally. Day after day he lay between two tanks of smelly developing fluid in a niche barely big enough for his body. It was impossible for him to keep his paws beneath him constantly and time after time I stepped on them. No yelping complaint—he would simply stand and accept my apology, lick my hand and lie down again.

That wonderful morning finally came. "Joe," said Miss Lee when she finished checking the X-rays I had just developed, "you're a good technician. Now you're ready to get a job."

Before the day was over I had followed her lead to the hospital in Port Chester. They needed me . . . I could begin the next day!

There was no way to hold down the excitement I felt, so after supper Rally and I headed outside for a romp. It was a great moment for us both. We were on our way to a new independence, earning our own way, really helping people. And this big shaggy bundle, bouncing and leaping at my side, had a lot to do with it all. I grabbed at the mop of hair that still seemed to nearly hide his eyes. "How come you think you can see for me, boy? You can't even see for yourself! Fetch it, Rally. Fetch!"

He dashed from my side in an exuberant charge after the play block. I heard him panting as he pounced on the target, and then his paws were scurrying again. His victory dance. A wide circle to impress me with his conquest before bringing the block back. The street. Never in the street, Rally!

The car's tires squealed as they swept around the corner. I felt . . . even before the impact, I knew with that awful sense of impending disaster Rally was going to be struck. I wanted to scream but nothing would come. And then there was that terrible sound as the car hit him, the sound of metal against bone and the horrible cry from Rally.

"Oh, no! NO!" I ran into the street where he lay whimpering. When I touched him, he raised his head, squirmed and tried to get up, but couldn't. I cried helplessly as I held his head in my lap.

She stood by my side; I could sense her there. "I'm sorry," she said. "I didn't see him." Then I heard the sound of her heels hurrying away. She was leaving us! Leaving Rally hurt so badly in the middle of the road! The car door opened. "I'm sorry." I heard her say again and the car raced away.

That night I lay awake in my bedroom, alone, without my dog. I thought about the next day, my first job at United Hospital. How could I make it without Rally? I'd pleaded to be allowed to stay with him overnight, but it wasn't possible. I remembered the way his legs were stiffening under the blanket toward the last. I was sure he was dying. Somehow that long night ended.

"Rally made it through the night," reported the veterinarian's wife when I called. "We were surprised, but he did."

I was elated almost beyond self-control. "He's alive!" I wanted the whole wide world to know the good news. Dad was waiting in the car to take me to work and now I was ready. So what if I was cane walking again for the first time in a long, long time? Rally was holding on!

It was 4:30 P.M. when my father picked me up again and we drove directly to the veterinarian's. There was a sudden, frightening chill as the doctor led us into his office and asked me to sit down. "Joe, Rally died at four this morning. I stayed with him through the night, but there was nothing I could do. His back was broken in two places."

"No!" I couldn't believe it. "He can't be! Your wife, she said . . ."

"She couldn't tell you when you called. I'm sorry, it may have been the wrong thing, but she was afraid. We knew you were just starting your new work today and didn't want to hurt you there." His voice broke. "I'm sorry, Joe."

I left his office locked in grief, unable even to thank him for staying up with Rally, doing his best. I felt drained and the tears wouldn't stop. Clenched tightly in a fist that I ground against my chest to try to hold back the pain was Rally's choker collar. Nothing, I knew, could ever be the same again.

For days I was numb to everything, even cruel to those most dear to me, who waited and watched . . . and understood. And then it happened. The agony quieted and the grief eased. I could only remember the many things Rally had done for me, the wonderful walks, the way he would tug to keep me upright when I slipped, the funny things . . . like the time Mother made me a sandwich and put it on the table while I was washing. When she turned to pour a glass of milk, Rally carried both the dish and sandwich to the living room and casually devoured my lunch.

Another time I attended a social function, looping Rally's leash around the leg of the table at which I was sitting. My date and I had scarcely joined the other couples out on the floor when we heard a strange scraping sound. Here came Rally to join us, unconcernedly pulling the table behind him.

———————————

I'll remember these things and ever so much more. He was so great, my wonderful Rally. He was my eyes with a waggin' tail.

HER BEST WORK

Howe Benning

*T*he little country school was a last resort for newly graduated Grace Archer. It was in a remote little village and it paid almost nothing—however, it was a job, a beginning, so she took it. Next year, she'd be in a real school!

But God had reasons for placing her there—reasons she gradually came to understand.

T he long years of study were over, and Grace Archer was graduated, with good rank and an honorable record.

Ever since she could remember, it had been her dream to win a place of honor and usefulness as a teacher, to be spoken of as a success, to gain a salary that should make petty economies unnecessary and permit her to give welcome gifts to the home circle or to gain glimpses of life at the seashore or in fine hotels, or even to enjoy a trip to Europe. Why not? Others had done so. And she meant to do good, to help her pupils, and to go down in their lives as an uplifting memory.

But the long vacation was nearly over, and no place had offered itself. Teachers' employment bureaus had swallowed up what little money she had and now had apparently forgotten her.

It was not until the very week before the opening of the schools that any position presented itself, and it was nothing at all like she had hoped for.

Up in a mountain town, ten miles from a railroad, nestled a small sleepy village with a school of three grades. The "high room" called in pupils from the country around, and required two teachers for its fifty or more pupils, ranging in age from fourteen to twenty. Grace Archer's name had been given to the school board, and she was offered a place at a salary of seven and one-half dollars a week.

"Ridiculous!" a friend responded; but Grace would not be "left out in the cold," as she expressed it; thus the soft hush of the mountain road, on a September day, gathered her into its heart as she came to the cluster of houses set as in a cup around a tiny park, with the white church spire, the two stores, and the two-story, gray-tinted school building. On the upper floor of this building were the assembly room and a long, narrow room for herself and her classes.

Here, as Grace Archer used to say in later years, began her "real education." They were not dull pupils that were sent into that long room, by any means. Many of them drove miles over the hills, studying their textbooks on the way, and were ready with questions that made of their teacher a night student as well as themselves.

With all her enthusiasm Grace entered into her new work. It was a very subtle delight to be the center of so much attention, and sometimes to have a hand slip into her own with the whispered words, "How did you ever happen to come up here, Miss Archer?"

She wondered at it herself, sometimes. She seemed to be of so much importance—her every wish deferred to, her opinion sought so constantly—that she concluded that her own worth in the world had been acknowledged. Yes, this year of probation, or beginning, was a wise thing, after all. She knew now that she could make a success as a teacher. The next fall should find her in more fitting surroundings.

She was standing by her window one night after school, when Allie, a girl of eighteen, the most brilliant and troublesome pupil in school, entered and walked to her side.

"Miss Archer, will you tell me how to become such a woman as you are?" she said simply.

In her longing to help this questioner the teacher forgot all shyness, and, before they separated, they knelt together, and the questioning soul was consecrated to the service of the Savior. That was the beginning of an awakening in the spiritual life of the school, for one after another came to the weekly meeting established by these two, asking, seeking, and finding. As a result, the small church in the village gathered new members and new courage, and the Sunday school woke to new life.

The year wore on to its closing. One night, the week before examinations, two letters came to the teacher. One was from the committee of her own school, asking her to resume her position for the coming year, at an increase of one dollar a week in salary. The other letter was from a trustee in a city school, who had visited the mountain town, and now offered her a position with twice her present salary. She could have a week to decide. But she knew that she did not need an hour. In her own mind the question was decided. She did not regret the year in the village school; she had learned many things. But now a suitable place had presented itself, and it would be foolish to let it pass.

With a strange reluctance, however, she said nothing of her decision to anyone. It was almost sunset on the day of the final examination. She had been listening to essays to be read in public on the morrow. She was alone in her room, and again Allie entered.

"Are you coming back next year, Miss Archer?" she asked.

"Probably not," was the reply.

"Then that finishes my education," the girl replied with a firm set to her lips.

"But your parents' wishes, Allie."

"I cannot help it. I am going into a store in the city, where I can go and see things. If you were here, I could stand remaining; but I will not come back here otherwise. So there!" And the door closed—not gently.

It opened again for a tall, ungainly fellow, with broad brow and earnest eyes. "Here is the geometry book you lent me, Miss Archer," he said. "I never could understand it before. You've made it plain as day. If I can have one more year with you—and it looks now as if I might—I think I'll be ready for college, and then I'll be ready for work. I mean to be a minister some day, Miss Archer. I never thought of it until you said, one day, that life ought to be given to what was worthwhile."

This time she had only a handclasp to give. Tears dimmed all the beauty of the green hillsides as she looked again from her window. But when she turned away at last, the decision was made to remain just where she was. "I have found my work here," she wrote that night to the trustee of the city school.

For four years Grace Archer remained faithfully at her place in the village. Then, when Allie returned from two years of seminary training, fitted to do good work, strong in character, and glad to remain with parents and in her own town, Miss Archer accepted the call to a larger school. Yet, after twenty years of the most successful teaching, she says today, "I feel that my best work was done in that quiet little village. My intimate association with small classes gave me a knowledge of character and human nature that I could never have won in the larger classrooms. The devotion of my pupils taught me unselfishness. If I were called upon now to forget any four years of my life, those spent in that hill-town schoolroom would be the last ones I could part with. For there I believe I received my own best lessons and came nearest to my own highest ideals."

ONE MORE
PRAYER

Ronald Boyd

Merlin was the most talked-about boy in the Academy, both by the students and by the faculty. Seemingly, he was almost always in hot water of some kind.

But everyone needs at least one friend, and Merlin found that in Roger, so the two boys decided to room together. Then came the turning point. Things were never the same afterwards. . . . For the rest of his life, Roger would wonder about the last words he ever received from Merlin.

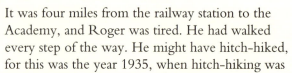It was four miles from the railway station to the Academy, and Roger was tired. He had walked every step of the way. He might have hitch-hiked, for this was the year 1935, when hitch-hiking was very popular; but Roger was both proud and bashful. He had just left the farm, at the age of sixteen, and sixteen years of farm life had made him quite independent. So he walked the four miles, carrying his heavy suitcase.

The Academy for which he was bound was beautifully situated on a knoll overlooking a wooded valley and a winding river below. The scene was especially welcome to Roger's tired eyes on the warm September afternoon of his arrival. Now to find the boys' dormitory and a good shower!

Over on the far side of the campus he saw a young man indifferently following a lawn mower. The young man seemed to resent the fact that the lawn mower must of necessity be pushed or it would not cut the grass. Roger advanced hesitantly toward the young man who had seen the stranger's approach and now was leaning leisurely on the handle of his machine, his hat cocked on the side of his head, a critical expression in his eye.

"My name's Roger Adams," said the new student, introducing himself.

There was a slight pause. "Mine's Merlin Philips; so what?"

Roger gulped; then he stammered, "I wonder if you could tell me where the boys' dormitory is?"

"Right over there," Merlin answered without hesitation, pointing to a large building across the field.

Roger's sixteen years of farm experience told him that the large building across the field was a cow barn, not a dormitory. Now, he had been taught to be courteous to strangers. He had also been taught tolerance; but tolerance is not usually the most strongly developed virtue found in young people. Back on the farm if a cow kicked him once, Roger overlooked it; but if she kicked him twice he usually retaliated with counter-measures. Roger was definitely a diamond in the rough.

And now, as he stood facing his newly made acquaintance, he was in a retaliating mood. The situation might have become serious had not Roger seen some young men entering a building near by. Assuming that this was the boys' home, he picked up his suitcase and disappeared into the building. Merlin resumed his position behind the lawn mower.

Merlin was the most talked-about student in the school, both in faculty meetings and in student conversations. He had arrived at the Academy a week early this year just to watch all the "freshies" come in. Last year he had been a freshman; but now he was a sophomore and really "knew his way around." Merlin was the school's number one problem. He had a good voice, but he refused to sing. He had a keen intellect, but he got the poorest grades in school. He was against everything. The faculty all agreed that Merlin was the most complicated and warped character they had ever dealt with. Among his many failings, his cutting sarcasm was the most pronounced, for he seemed to think that every occasion demanded a sarcastic remark. Everyone in school, both faculty members and students, had at one time or another fallen victim to his stinging remarks.

Every school has its problem students, but when they are called in for discipline they usually become somewhat repentant and promise to try to improve. Not so with Merlin. He talked right back to his teachers and the rest of the faculty, telling them all "where to get off." If he had been a less-complicated character, the faculty would have expelled him long before; but Merlin's case challenged his teachers. So they kept him in school and heaped free labor upon him as punishment for his misdemeanors.

Merlin would probably not have treated Roger with quite such rudeness upon their first meeting had he not been in an ugly humor. But the second day after his return to school he had been into mischief, and now he was doing free labor mowing the lawn, and Merlin hated free labor.

During his freshman year, Roger saw very little of Merlin. This was partly due to Roger's determination to avoid him as much as possible and to the fact that both boys worked their entire way and were kept busy. Fortunately, they worked in different departments.

Roger made many friends; Merlin alienated many would-be friends.

The school year went by and summer came. Both boys decided to stay and work at the school to earn credit for the following year. It was during this summer that their friendship started. Roger was transferred to Merlin's department, and the two boys worked side by side. Merlin was continually in trouble; and Roger, who always had a soft spot in his heart for the underdog, decided to befriend him.

Human nature demands that every individual have someone in whom to confide, and Merlin was no exception. He began confiding in his new-found friend, especially after the two boys began rooming together. Roger learned that his roommate was an orphan who did not even know who his parents were, and that from infancy he had been kept by friends. The more Merlin told him, the more sympathetic Roger became, until finally he not only became his staunch friend, but he was determined that everyone else should befriend Merlin also.

All during the year that followed, Roger kept turning the old saying over in his mind: "Birds of a feather flock together," and he wondered whether that was what the faculty and students were saying about him since he had become a close friend to Merlin. Roger tried hard during that year to get others to befriend his roommate, and he succeeded to some extent. His own close friends accepted Merlin into their circle more or less as a favor to Roger, for Merlin hadn't changed much. He was still a sophomore, having failed or dropped most of his courses during the past year.

But Roger had changed and was still changing, for the diamond in the rough was becoming polished. Merlin's sarcasm no longer bothered him, because he had educated himself to rise above it. In fact, Merlin became his hobby. He tried every method, he approached from every avenue, in his attempt to help his roommate to acquire a healthy philosophy of life. Sometimes they lay awake talking till well past midnight, Roger trying tactfully to help his friend see his mistakes. He prayed for him silently every night; but he saw very little change in Merlin's attitude.

There were a few times, however, when Merlin seemed almost to have decided to take his stand for right and become a Christian. One winter evening during Roger's junior year, he strolled into the room and called the usual, "Hi, roommate!" There was no answer. Merlin was moodily gazing out the window at the drizzling rain. "What's the matter, pal?"

"Aw, what's the use? You remember that mess I was in last week?"

Roger remembered, all right. The week before, Merlin and some of the other fellows had been found smoking, and today the faculty was meeting to decide what action should be taken. Merlin expected that they would expel him. Oh, well, he could never figure out why he "hung around this joint" anyway—let them kick him out.

"The principal called me in today," continued Merlin; "I expected that he would tell me that the faculty had decided to expel me."

Merlin hesitated.

"Well?"

"They haven't been planning to expel me at all; they've been *praying* for me!" Merlin choked, and tears came to his eyes. "A fellow doesn't have a chance against people like that." He swallowed.

Roger moved over and put his arm around his friend's shoulder. "Why not turn over a new leaf, pal?" he asked. "Tonight at evening vespers, if there's a testimony service, why not stand with the rest of the students?"

Merlin did not promise, but he remained quiet and thoughtful. The speaker at vespers talked on the forgiving love of Jesus. He read from the Bible: "Come unto Me, all ye that labor and are heavy laden, and I will give you rest;" and "Though your sins be as scarlet, they shall be as white as snow." When he made a call for consecration, Merlin stood with the rest. He uttered a short testimony and sat down. Roger felt a surge of happiness, and yet—he wondered. That night he offered a fervent prayer that God would especially strengthen Merlin in this supreme struggle.

"I'm not going to church today," Merlin said the next morning; "I don't feel well."

Roger's spirits sank, but he said nothing, for if Merlin were going to live a Christian life, the final decision would have to be made by him, not Roger.

When Roger returned to the room after church, Merlin was gone. He was gone all day. About three o'clock in the morning

Roger was awakened by a slight shuffling sound. Merlin was stealthily tiptoeing into the room.

"Hi, roommate," whispered Roger.

Merlin was startled, but he regained his composure defiantly. "Huh," he sneered, "waiting up for me like the dear old gray-haired mother in the storybooks. 'Oh, where is my wandering boy tonight?'"

"Pipe down and go to bed," answered Roger.

But Merlin had to get it off his chest. "I went to the big city today, and I took in every show in town; I had a drink and smoked a couple of packs of cigarettes. So what! I'm rotten clear through, and religion wasn't made for me."

Roger sighed inwardly. Merlin had failed. Those habits which are incompatible with Christian character were forged about him like bands of steel. Bad habits are so hard to break, and one bad habit always breeds another. This boy certainly had his share of them.

It was a personal defeat for Roger, and he could not help feeling resentful toward his roommate. During the following weeks Merlin slid back into the same old rut, and Roger became completely disgusted and finally made arrangements with the dean to move into another room. When Merlin came in that evening, Roger was just gathering up the last of his belongings.

Merlin regarded his roommate questioningly. But Roger didn't wait for a verbal question; he blurted out, "I'm through, Merlin. I've been a friend to you and done everything I could to help you. I've prayed for you every day, but it hasn't done any good. I guess there's nothing more I can do for you."

"OK, wise guy," said Merlin as he turned his back and walked away.

In the weeks that followed, Merlin was a lone wolf. He

avoided everyone, and no one seemed to mind. Roger's heart went out to him, but he said nothing, for he felt that his time had been wasted. Had he been a little older, he probably would have been more patient and not have forsaken his friend, realizing that there is a crisis hour in every life before the final break. But patience is another virtue that is seldom strongly developed in youth.

Several weeks passed; then one day Roger's door opened, and in walked Merlin.

"I'm leaving school," he stated with studied indifference. "I've joined the Navy, and I have a little keepsake for you. I've cut a coin in two at the middle. You take one half and I'll take the other, and we'll keep them as souvenirs of each other—till we meet again." With these words he turned and walked out.

Roger finished the Academy and went on to college. School life was so crowded that he seldom thought of his former friend; however, they did correspond occasionally.

One day in the late summer of 1941, Roger received a letter from Hawaii. It was from Merlin. He had been transferred to Pearl Harbor, and was aboard the U.S. destroyer *Shaw*. The letter was short, but Roger was impressed by its contents.

Merlin had written: "I'm glad you like it so well at college. I wish I had stuck; but I guess I just didn't have what it takes. I'll never forget the time you told me that you had been praying for me, but it hadn't done any good, and that there was nothing more you could do for me. You know, Roger, one more prayer might have done it."

A short time later came December 7, and the attack on Pearl Harbor. When the reports came out in the papers, Roger read in full headlines: "Three Thousand Officers and Men Killed, Three Destroyers Lost." Among the ships lost was the *Shaw*.

Roger was stunned. Memories flooded his mind, and he searched out the little half coin that Merlin had given him as a keepsake. He fingered the coin thoughtfully. *Till we meet again,* Merlin had said; *one more prayer might have done it.*

THE LAME DUCK

Thomas A. Curry

Freshman David Haines was a friendless loner—and he liked it that way. Nobody but nobody would ever break through his defenses. Pity—he'd endured enough of it. But that pesky Paul Miller; if he'd only quit knocking on his door! Anybody else would get the message—and leave him alone.

n his eighteenth year, his first year at college, David Haines had not a friend among his many classmates. It was not the fault of the latter. Several had tried to be chummy with him, had endeavored to get beyond the acquaintance stage, where they simply nodded and passed a word about the weather or the professors, and so on. But David was morose, unbending—polite and cool. He seldom smiled.

He was a tall, well-proportioned fellow, was David. His hair was dark and his eyes black—a good-looking chap, all around, except—it was the "except" which made David as he was— except that he walked with a limp! In his fourteenth year David Haines's right foot had been badly injured; and when he got about again he was irreparably lame.

Since the day when, thus handicapped, he had returned to school, David had been a "lone wolf." He brooded a great deal, which is bad for anyone; he thought people laughed at him, which is worse; and worst of all, he had grown to dislike his fellows.

He was naturally a good student. And because of his affliction, he never took part in athletics or social affairs. In high school he had always been excused from physical culture classes; and in college he had started out in the same way. He intended to concentrate on studying and reading, and the rest of it he could do without, as far as he was concerned.

He roomed alone. He had insisted on that. He didn't want anyone bothering him and pitying him. That was pride, that last, for he felt that if any fellow were to pity him, it would be worse than being laughed at. So he stumped around, his eyes down, his shoulders stooped, from class to class. When some classmate tried to talk to him, he nodded uninterestedly—he felt that he was being pitied or patronized; when they asked him to come out for the glee club, he refused, though he had a good baritone voice.

From his study window he was forced to look out upon the campus where fifty or sixty of his mates frolicked and played in the cool autumn afternoons. And in the gymnasium—where David had been only once, when, as required, he had reported there the first day—basketball and gymnastics went on. And below the gymnasium, David knew there was a swimming pool. Not that he cared. He had been excused from physical exercise by Dr. James, the head of the department.

The college, Colby, had about eight hundred students. They were proud of their athletic prowess. In David's mathematics class were two varsity football players and a basketball captain. David was an advanced student in several subjects and couldn't help but notice that athletes, as a rule, seemed to struggle scholastically. Beside him, in his English class, sat Paul Miller, whom David knew to be on the swimming team.

Miller was a big, light-haired youth, with a sunny smile and a pleasant voice. He was in his second year and taking almost the same course as David, though they were in different sections in all classes save English.

"Looks as if we'd have a hard time with old Chip-ear," said Miller, indicating the professor. "He's said to be the hardest marker in the col'. I never had him before."

David shrugged. "Perhaps you'll have trouble," he said coolly, "but I don't expect to. I can pass any course they can fix up for the average dumb-bell."

Miller's smile faded. He tried again. "Do you live in New York?" he asked. "I come from Philadelphia."

"No, I don't live in New York."

David turned away and pretended to be writing in his

note-book. The professor was running over the list of reading matter for the term.

After class, David limped out, eyes down, trying to avoid the evident friendliness of Miller, who walked beside him.

"Going to have a great football team this year," began Miller.

David displayed no interest.

"Got the whole team from last year except the quarterback," continued Miller. "We ought to beat Kennedy this year. Do you do any swimming?"

"No," said David. "I'm not interested in athletics. I'm lame." And leaving the embarrassed Miller, he limped away to his room.

Miller made several more attempts to be friendly, all of which David squelched. He felt that the big chap was sorry for him, and he began to dislike Miller.

David's mother was dead. His father was a busy man, and David saw him only when he was home during holidays, so that he literally was alone in the world. And he didn't care—at least, he told himself that he didn't.

Miller still kept trying to make friends with him, asking to borrow David's note-book, or trying to talk about the triumphs of the football team. No rebuffs seemed to do any good.

It was toward the end of October. David had been sitting in his room, reading, when a knock came. He was surprised, for no one ever came to see him. With a slight frown, he limped to the door and opened it. There stood Paul Miller.

"Hello, old top," said Miller, breezily. "Just dropped in to say howdy."

"Oh—come in."

David stared at Miller and Miller shifted uneasily. "Mind if I sit down for a while?" he asked.

David shook his head, and Miller sat down.

"Why don't you ever come out with the boys?" began Miller. "I haven't seen you at all, and you've been here six weeks now, Haines. Ought to mix in a bit. Good for you to make contacts. Don't you get lonely?"

"No, I never get lonely. When I was in high school, the fellows used to call me 'Limpety,'" he added irrelevantly. "That's funny, isn't it? To be laughed at—or to be pitied and patronized." And he glared at Miller.

"Nobody's patronizing you," the latter said uneasily. "I like you, Haines, that's all. That's the way it is: you like someone and you try to make friends with 'em. But you seem to think no one is worthwhile. Well, you're mistaken. You ought to have friends. You never stick your nose outside of your room except for classes and meals."

David determined to show Miller once and for all that he did not encourage callers. "And why should that trouble you?" he said bitterly. "It's my business if I don't choose to mix with every Tom, Dick, and Harry that comes along."

"No, you don't mean that," said Miller, quietly. "I hate to see you so foolish, Haines. Why don't you make the best of things? You could have a good time, even if you are—"

David rose quickly. "I hope you'll excuse me. I've a great deal of work to do."

Miller got slowly to his feet. He was flushing hotly. "I'm sorry, Haines. I didn't mean to force myself on you."

For several minutes after he had gone, David stood with clenched fists, his anger at Miller's intrusion taking complete control of him. Then a queer little lump rose in his throat. He fought it down.

"Serves him right," he muttered. "He won't try it again."

And at the thought, he was amazed to find just a touch of

sorrow. He called himself all kinds of a fool and went back to his books.

To his intense surprise, Miller did come again. It was a week later, and in the afternoon the schedule for the mid-term examinations had been posted. David was studying analytical geometry, with a compass and drawing-board at his elbow. Someone knocked, and David knew instinctively it was Miller. He waited a moment, then went to the door and threw it open.

"Well?" he inquired. He had been cutting Miller as obviously as possible when they met on the campus or in class. Miller had nodded gravely and that was all; now he had several books under his arm.

He stepped into the room and shut the door behind him. He did not sit down, but laid the books on the arm of David's big chair.

"I've come on business," he said quietly. "I want to know if you can give me a lift in some of my studies. I—"

"Really, I don't see why you should bother me," broke in David.

But Miller raised his hand. "I'll be glad to pay you if you'll help me along a little," he said. "If I fail, I won't be able to swim on the team, and the team needs me. I wouldn't trouble you; I could go to one of the other fellows I know better, but—well, the truth is, Haines, I know that if you tutor me, you won't say anything to anybody about it. I'd hate to have people saying I was stupid. You understand?"

A queer little smile flitted across his face. A strange emotion flooded over David. There stood Miller, the big fellow, a worried look in his blue eyes, appealing to *him!* David realized that he felt sorry for Paul Miller.

"Why, surely!" he said quickly. "I'll—I'll be glad to help you, old man. And don't talk about paying me—I'll be glad to do it for nothing."

"That's awfully good of you." Miller smiled, holding out his hand. Embarrassed, yet with a flood of happiness in his heart, David took it.

"There's analytical geometry," said Miller, quickly. "Also, I wish you'd help me get the differences between the Romans and Greeks. That's in our English, you remember. And French— what French are you taking—French B?"

David nodded. "I think I can help you in those three. That's all?"

"That's enough, isn't it?" grinned Miller.

David laughed, and Paul joined him. With a new joy in studying, David set about explaining the complexities of analytical geometry to an admiring and attentive listener.

When Paul left that night at ten o'clock, David limped down the corridor with him, shouting good night as Miller clattered down the stairs to his room, two floors below—really happy for the first time since he had come to Colby, or since his accident, for that matter. Miller and he had chatted for ten minutes when they had finished studying, and Miller had told him about the swimming team and the excitement of it all. A longing to be in it swept over David.

It was the next morning that he got the letter. It was an official notice from Dr. James, the physical-education director: "Every student is required to swim half a mile before he will be allowed to receive his diploma. It is customary to pass this test during the freshman year."

David tossed the letter into the waste-basket. Dr. James had excused him from such fooleries.

But on the following Monday he received another

communication: "We have not heard from you yet concerning your swimming test. Kindly call at the gymnasium office at once. Alfred D. James."

David called that afternoon, in an injured mood. Dr. James, a short, powerful little man, gave him a friendly nod.

"I've had a couple of letters from you in regard to the swimming test," began David. "You excused me from physical education."

"Yes, I know I did. But you'd better take the swimming test. It will be good for you. Can't you swim?"

"A little. But not half a mile."

"Well, the coach will help you. You practice daily and soon you'll be able to do it in record time."

Dr. James turned away as though the interview were closed.

"But—Dr. James—I'm lame. I can't swim. I haven't been in the water since—since my foot was hurt. I—"

"Haines," said the doctor, regarding him steadily, "if I thought you couldn't do it, I'd not insist. But you can't evade everything by pleading your injury. You can take the swimming test well enough."

David flushed hotly. "If you think—," he began. Then he rose, and without another word stalked from the room with as much dignity as he could muster.

He was very angry. He brooded all day in his room. At night after supper, Miller came, and after he had tried in vain to keep his trouble to himself, David told him what had occurred.

"Why, the old sea-hawk!" exclaimed Miller, sympathetically. "So he told you you'd have to take the swimming test, did he? What are you going to do?"

"I don't know. I might go to the Dean. I'd like to tell James where to get off. But I suppose the only thing to do is to go ahead and swim."

"That's the spirit!" Miller had a sudden inspiration. "Say, old man—why don't you let me help you with your swimming—I mean, it'd only be a little return for what you're doing for me. What say?"

David thought for a moment. "That will be great, Paul. But—don't think me foolish—I'd just as soon swim when there aren't many people around."

"All right. Tomorrow at five-thirty. What say? Won't be anybody there but the coach, Bill Carstairs. The practice is over by then."

The next afternoon, David limped to the pool below the gymnasium. He was angry, very angry with Dr. James; but he had determined that nothing would induce him to ask any more favors of the little man.

He was surprised to find how pleasant the water was, and what a sense of exhilaration he got from splashing about in the shallow end of the pool. His muscles were soft from the disuse; he had taken no hard exercise for years. Beside Miller's sleek, shining, well-muscled body, his looked below par.

"You've got a swimmer's natural build," Miller said, as he swam up. "Let's see what you can do in the way of a stroke."

David swam two or three yards of the breast stroke.

"That's the best you can do?" called Miller.

"Yes," answered David. He felt a little ashamed, but soon became interested in watching Miller.

"Look at me!" shouted Miller.

Launching himself into position for the crawl stroke, the swimmer passed back and forth with slow, easy motion, legs churning the water and arms reaching out.

"That's the only stroke worth bothering with," said Miller, stopping. "Come on now! I'm going to hold you while you go through the motions. Flat on the water, your nose just submerged. Turn your head to breathe as your right arm comes back. Inhale through your mouth, exhale through your nose, under water. Right."

His eyes smarting from the water and with a sensation of drowning, David did as he was bid. He didn't think he was going to like the crawl; but he tried, with all his energy, to follow Miller's directions.

"Kick from the hip. Just keep your knees slightly bent—that's the way. Toes extended and slightly turned in. Kick like blazes. Splash the water. Right."

Inside of an hour, David had been told the many points to remember when swimming the crawl. But swimming it was a different matter. It took him three weeks of daily practice before the unused muscles began to limber up enough to allow him to swim the stroke. But he kept on.

Every week-day David went to the pool and swam under Miller's guidance. His lameness did not hamper him; in fact, when he was in the water he forgot that he was lame. He was able to swim well, and could go thirty lengths of the pool at a slow pace.

"Now," said Miller, one day after watching him, "you can pass that test easily. But you're not going to quit swimming, are you?"

"Quit? Certainly. Why should I keep on?"

"Why, I don't know. I thought you liked it. Why don't you try out for the team?"

David laughed. He was surprised as well as amused. "*I?* Try out for the team? And be laughed at?"

"Laughed at, nothing! Nobody will laugh at you. We're short

of two-twenty men, and you've picked up the stroke in very quick time—maybe not in championship form, but well enough to keep on. The season opens Saturday, and we swim against eight colleges. Why not try out?"

David shook his head. "No, Paul. I'm going to take the test tomorrow and then I'll be through. You've been mighty good to bother so much with me, though."

Next afternoon, Carstairs, the coach, passed Dave in the swimming test. He watched David as the latter made his way up and down the pool. When David was through, he called to him. David limped over.

"Nice stroke you're developing," said Carstairs, gruffly. "Why don't you try out for the team? Miller told me to watch you and see if you weren't worthwhile. I think you are."

It was the way he said it that caused David to hesitate. If the man had come over to him, instead of calling him, or had been very kind, David would have refused at once. But there was something genuine about Carstairs.

"I don't know. I hadn't thought of the team."

"Show up tomorrow at four. Team practice then," said the coach, turning away as though the business were settled.

And to Miller's obvious delight, David appeared at four and stiffly shook hands with the members of the team. They were nice clean-cut, smiling fellows. They paid no attention to his bad foot, but complimented him on his stroke and discussed with him the intricacies and complexities of the crawl.

Later on, the manager called to him, and, when David went over, issued him a swimming suit. "Practice every day at four," he was told.

For three more weeks he went to the pool every day, limping at Miller's side till they plunged into the water. He didn't quite know how to act with his fellows: it had been so long since he had been on friendly terms with anyone but Miller. He stood to one side and listened while the others joked and laughed and played.

Two Saturday nights, when there were meets, David sat on the sidelines with the other substitutes and watched his team win. And the third Saturday the coach called him aside before the meet started.

"I want you to swim as second man in the two-twenty," ordered Carstairs. "Johnson is out, sick. Now go to it."

David's heart beat rapidly as he wriggled into his suit. Things seemed hazy, as though he were dreaming. He was to swim for the team! For the team? For the college—Colby. His heart leaped madly. He sat down on the narrow bench and put his head in his hands. Presently Miller came over and sat beside him.

"Carstairs tells me you're swimming with me. I knew you'd make it, old man. Don't forget to breathe well every stroke. And don't roll too much."

David could not recall ever having been so excited as when the two-twenty was announced and his name was called as the second Colby man. He limped to the end of the pool, trembling. He could see the spectators through a cloud, and dimly hear their yells as they encouraged the men.

"Swimming for Colby, Miller and—Haines!" He felt the announcer slap him on the shoulder.

Then: "On your marks—get set—*Bang!*"

A swift take-off, pushing from the end of the pool. He felt the water close over his body, and then, in the heat of contest, he forgot himself and his lameness. Nothing counted now but winning. On his right, as he breathed, he could see Miller foaming along; on his left he knew were their two opponents.

On the eighth lap he glanced over and saw that Miller was leading him by several feet. He increased the momentum of his stroke and put his tired muscles into a last effort.

Then someone pulled him out of the pool and patted him on the back. He wondered if he had come in very far behind the others.

"Good work, old scout!" cried Miller. "Not so bad."

"Result of two-twenty swim: Miller, Colby, first. Lewis, Princeton, second. Haines, Colby, third."

He had taken a place. In his first meet he had won a point for Colby—his college! And he had won something for her. A great happiness surged in his heart.

"Attaboy!" said Carstairs, as David staggered past him on the way to the dressing-room.

Paul awaited him at the door. "Coming in?" he asked.

"I guess not," said David. "I believe I'll watch the hundred."

Miller passed into the room. Then Dave decided he'd better dress and get warm. As he started to enter the room, he heard a friend's voice.

"He sure was a hard proposition. It was a job getting him out. But he's a good swimmer, and he's worth every bit of it, Doc."

Doc?

"He was sore at me, too. I'd have let him off if you hadn't asked me not to." It was the voice of Dr. James!

Suddenly David realized they were talking about him. It had been a "frame-up" then, between Miller and Dr. James, to get him out of his shell! He was about to rush in and denounce them; but he paused, for in his brain still echoed those wonderful words: *Haines, Colby, third!*

He walked into the dressing-room, smiling. "I'm obliged to you, Dr. James. You've made me see how foolish I was—you and Paul. I heard what you said—and I only hope you don't think I'm still the way I was."

They shook hands, the doctor cordially and Paul with a delighted grin. Presently the rest of the team came in, and they formed a happy, chattering group. Some were tired out, some were jubilant winners; but all were Colby men and David's mates. Unconsciously, David found himself talking.

"You swam mighty well," said little Brown, who had taken first place in the fifty. "If you hadn't been so slow on the turns, I believe you'd have beaten old man Miller here. He's a broken-down truck-horse anyway."

Paul tossed his wet suit at Brown. "Go home and grow up," he said.

"And the old lame duck here!" cried Brown, slapping David on the back; "he's the boy! Third place isn't bad for a beginner, let me tell you."

Lame duck! David laughed. It was funny to have a nickname like all the rest.

It was Brown who, a little later, enlightened him further. "I wish I could keep up with my studies the way you and Miller do," he said, as he and David walked across the campus together after the meet. "I'm getting down in my math."

"Maybe I can help you," said Dave. "I'd be glad to."

"Thanks. I'll be around. Old Miller is some scholar, believe me."

"Is he? I didn't know he got on so well."

"No?" said Brown, surprised. "Why, last year he was one of the highest in the class."

And suddenly Dave, with a great flood of affection for his pal, saw it all.

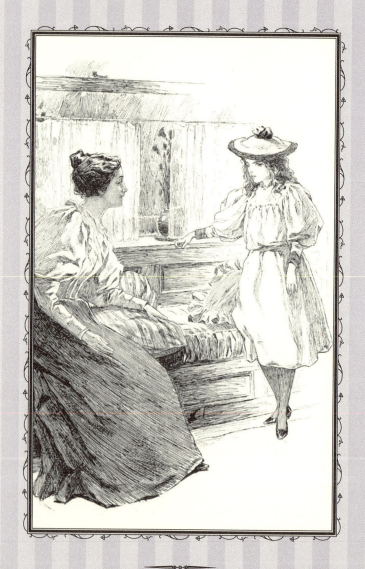

DEMENTIA PRAECOX

Della Dimmitt

$\mathcal{B}$eatta Marsh was afflicted with an overdose of noblesse oblige, as was the crowd of girls she associated with. Only girls from the "best families" were permitted to be part of their exclusive circle of friends. Well-traveled Cousin Marcella, with a little collusion from Mother, set about to bring democracy back to the little town.

ousin Marcella, I'm going to entertain for you."
Beatta Marsh tried to say it casually, just as she had
been trying for weeks past to say over and over to
herself: "It's only a little informal luncheon, girls, to
meet my cousin, Marcella Marsh, who is just back from a trip
around the world."

Unaware of the pent-up emotions boiling beneath these simply
spoken words, Miss Marsh, who happened to be Bee Marsh's
father's cousin and near his age, objected: "Oh, don't, Bee! Just
being with your mother and you is a pleasure enough for me."

"But, Cousin Marcella," exclaimed Bee, acute dismay in her
high-pitched girlish voice, "what will folks think of us if we keep
you all to ourselves? Besides, the girls are simply wild to meet
you. It isn't every day a person from New York who has circumnavigated the globe"—"circumnavigated" being a trifle vague in
meaning to Bee—"comes to Havenhill, and I owe it to my circle
of friends that they be given an opportunity of meeting you.
Can't you see how it is? Why, I've counted on giving this luncheon for you for more than a year, and the girls would *never* forgive me if I let it fall through now."

"Who are these girls you are so anxious to stand in with, Bee?"
Miss Marsh asked that quite as though she and Bee's mother
had never had any conversation regarding the social life in
Havenhill as related to Bee, when only the day before Mrs.
Marsh had said with despair in her voice: "They are apes, silly
apes; that's what these schoolgirls are. They dress like fashion
plates, and where they get their ideas about dress and social con-
ventions I'm sure I don't know. You would think they were all
scions of royalty to hear them discuss their involved and absurd
'social standards,' things of which we in our day never dreamed.
They are even trying to train the boys to ask them two weeks in

advance for a date, and they expect the boys to furnish flowers and taxis for their parties, until the poor, bewildered lads don't know what to make of it all.

"Oh! don't say that we poor parents are to blame for this state of affairs, Marcella. We know well enough what is wrong—'dementia praecox' [adolescent craziness] is what Dave calls it; but spanking girls and putting them to bed, as would have been done in our time, is not a method we modern mothers dare employ. And as for this luncheon, you may as well submit to it with what grace you can muster. It will cost a lot of money and days of work for me, but Bee's social prestige would be forever extinguished if she did not give it."

And it was with those strong words running through her mind that Miss Marsh had asked that question of Bee.

"Why, they're the nicest girls in town, Cousin Marcella; and they're very exclusive."

"Exclusive? Now, just what do you mean by that, Bee?"

"Why—why, they're girls from the first families; girls who know how to dress and how to entertain, who always do the correct thing, and—and who are up in literature, don't you know?"

"Well, if they're up in literature," said Cousin Marcella dryly, "one certainly ought to know them. Where are they in school?"

"Oh, they are all in my class in high school."

"And does your circle include all the girls in your class, Bee?"

"Oh! not all, Cousin Marcella. You know that would not be possible in just a public school like Havenhill High. You see everybody—just everybody—goes to high school. It isn't the select few such as we'll find when we enroll over at the academy."

"Well, I seem to have been gone from my country a longer time than I had supposed," remarked Cousin Marcella. "When I left, we had a democracy. Now, it appears, we have a limited aristocracy. I like democracies, Bee, where everybody, whether in school or out, gets recognition. Now, if you care to invite *all* the girls in your class—every one of them, mind you—I believe that I shall enjoy meeting them."

"But that is impossible," said Bee almost tearfully. "You don't understand, Cousin Marcella. Why, a washerwoman's daughter is in the class, and an Italian girl whose father works in the mines, and another girl whose mother has a rag carpet—a common rag carpet—in her best room. They've only lately moved here, and we don't know a thing about what kind of folks they are. Why, the girls would be horrified to have their names go into the paper with those girls. The paper always asks for our guest list."

"Well, then, I see no way out except to abandon your plan of entertaining for me altogether, for I am opposed to slighting any one of those girls in your class"; and there was a finality about Cousin Marcella's unruffled voice that precluded further argument.

Abandon the luncheon! Cousin Marcella evidently did not know Bee, nor the unalterableness of her course when her mind was set on anything. Since there was no escape from it, she gave her invitations, excluding none in the class; but to the inner circle she painstakingly explained her reasons for so doing, adding that Cousin Marcella, like all geniuses—how surprised Cousin Marcella would have been to know that she was one!—had her eccentricities; and the girls, in view of the desirability of acquainting themselves with so traveled a genius, graciously consented to honor the luncheon with their presence.

"But I wouldn't give out the guest list, Bee," one prudent girl urged. "Just say it was limited to close friends of the hostess, or to those composing the younger set, or something nice and vague like that. Personally, I like 'younger society set' best. That's what all the real citified papers say."

The excitement occasioned by the coming luncheon penetrated into many Havenhill homes, but in none was there more anxious discussion as to the proper raiment than in that of Mrs. Leary, the washerwoman. At length, the mother, planning a surprise for Annie yet fearful of making a mistake, opened her heart to Mrs. Marsh. "And will you tell me if these is good enough for my Annie to wear to your Beatta's luncheon?" and as she spoke, she unrolled a pair of expensive silk stockings.

"They will probably go without milk for a month to pay for them," said Mrs. Marsh in telling Marcella of the incident; "and it all comes from a set of foolish schoolgirls getting the upper hand and insisting on having things other girls cannot afford. I wanted to cry when I saw her poor, rough hands unrolling those stockings. I am pinning my faith on you, Marcella, to give this town some sort of a shake-up that will re-establish the fine and sweet simplicity that made us the women we are today. If you succeed in doing it, you will earn the gratitude of the troubled mothers who are at their wits' end in trying to stem the tide of extravagance and folly that is simply ruining the atmosphere of Havenhill."

The day of the luncheon came, and to all outward appearances Marcella was serenely indifferent to the general overturning of the universe in anticipation of the momentous event. She walked all morning through the old lanes and byways of the sprawlingly pretty old college town where her happy girlhood had been spent, renewing acquaintance with the townspeople, many of whom retained lively recollections of her as a winsome slip of a girl. At the appointed hour she came downstairs, having selected from an abundant wardrobe the simplest of pink ginghams set off by rows of pearl buttons.

Beatta crimsoned, but Cousin Marcella was not the sort of person one cared to advise in the matter of dress. The girls would just have to set that down as another of her eccentricities, and await another opportunity of seeing any of the wonderful gowns Bee had been at pains to describe to the younger society set.

Somewhat hesitatingly, Bee handed her guest of honor the elaborate corsage bouquet ordered expressly from the greenhouse for her. Cousin Marcella graciously accepted it, and extracting a single rose, thrust the rest into a vase, although it was carrying coals to Newcastle, so profusely were the rooms decorated with expensive cut flowers.

Hot and worried by endless directions from her demanding daughter, Mrs. Marsh stayed out in the kitchen; indeed, Bee seemed not to care about having her mother receive the guests with her. There were little round biscuits to make and put in the oven at the exact moment; and the patty-shells must be filled with the creamed mushrooms; the salad must not be made until the instant it was to be served; and Mother must please remember that nobody served with cereal, cream that wasn't whipped.

But Cousin Marcella, entirely oblivious of the inappropriateness of a gingham dress at so formal a function, was at her most charming best when the guests began to arrive. The members of that closed corporation, the younger society set, were easily discerned. All wore highly decorative frocks and smart kid gloves reaching to their elbows.

Cousin Marcella at once enchanted them, saying the appropriate thing to each and scattering her smiles impartially about on all. She talked with the Italian girl in her own musical tongue, the others listening quite breathlessly; then, turning, she explained that they were speaking of the glories of Rome, which had been the birthplace of little Angela's mother. "Tell your mother for me," she said brightly to the miner's daughter, "that I mean to pay her a visit soon. It may be that we have mutual friends in the city we both love." And Angela's kindling eyes told of the joy of one who unexpectedly finds a friend in a lonely land.

"And this is Miss Carola Gilmer next," Bee said; and Cousin Marcella's quick ear noted the same cool edge that had been in Bee's voice when presenting the Italian girl. She found confronting her, the last of the line, a slim maiden with adorable yellow pigtails that contrasted oddly with deep-brown eyes. She wore a simple gown of sheer blue wash fabric, and no gloves or ornaments of any kind.

Ah! the laundress's daughter; and, thinking that, Cousin Marcella gave the little warm hand an extra squeeze.

"My dear," she said radiantly, "you bring back my youth"— she paused in sudden bewilderment—"why, where *have* I seen you before? Who is it you look like? Who is your mother, child?"

"Mrs. Gilmer," laughed Carola shyly.

"But who was she before she was Mrs. Gilmer? Tell me quick."

Little Carola hesitated; the color flamed up in the honest girlish face turned pleadingly up at the fascinating Miss Marsh.

"Mamma would rather folks wouldn't know—just yet," she said simply.

The young ladies in the kid gloves ceased their conversation.

A mystery—something hidden—something disgraceful, no doubt; how very shocking! This was what they telegraphed with their eyes to one another.

Fully aware of this extraordinary little byplay, Miss Marsh

stood stock-still, amazement in her eyes; then something—perhaps the pigtails with their oddly familiar old-fashioned look, or else the leaf-brown eyes—stirred a memory. Suddenly she began to laugh, mirthfully, mischievously, as a girl laughs.

"Do you live in the little green-shuttered house at the very end of Crabapple Lane?" she asked, in a kind of whirl.

"Yes, Miss Marsh."

"And is there a rag carpet on the floor of that best room still?"

"Yes, Miss Marsh."

Cousin Marcella swiftly seized Carola's shapely head, sunlit pigtails and all, and rapturously kissed her.

"Girls!"—she turned dramatically, a daring purpose forming in her mind—"who of you want to go with me to fetch Carola Gilmer's mother? I must see her before I'm an hour older. Follow the leader!" and seizing Carola's hand, off she scurried, the panels of her pink gingham flying like banners in the fresh spring wind.

And they followed; oh, yes! they followed like the sheep they were, and as folks anywhere and everywhere always did follow whenever Marcella Marsh led. In a very few moments the door of the green-shuttered house at the tip end of Crabapple Lane was flung unceremoniously and widely open on a petite woman in a quaint mobcap sitting placidly at a desk and industriously scratching away on some long, loose strips of paper.

The writing one looked up in astonishment, and saw a conspicuously tall and handsome woman in pink gingham on the threshold.

"For the land's sake! if it isn't Mark Marsh!"

With a rush the two ran into each other's arms.

"Why, I thought you were at 'the antipathies,' Mark," exclaimed the lady of the mobcap, recovering first. "Just be seated—on the floor or anywhere."

Cousin Marcella paused long enough to wave affably toward the following she had drawn within. Then thrusting the lady of the mobcap back into her desk-chair and ensconcing herself on a little old faded footstool, she drew a long, ecstatic breath.

"I might have known it was you I saw this morning bending over Aunt Polly's tulip bed. Now, when will all those gay ladies in the flaming satin petticoats be up and in bloom? And when— oh! when can I come and sleep three in a bed once more up in that unfinished attic room, and talk till two in the morning, and listen to the rain pouring in sheets on the shingles just above our heads?"

"When it rains, Mark. We'll roast apples here on the hearth, too; and maybe we can induce 'Josie Cottontop' to come and turn the apples as he used to do; and 'Daisy Marsh' must come, too, and stretch those long legs of his out toward the flames, and tell us another ghost story while the apples sputter and bake."

With that for a starter, the rich stream of talk flowed on, one delightful incident following another of school days long past— mellow recollections that lived again in the retelling; and running through it all were the names of staid and substantial citizens whose scrapes and escapades sent the now breathlessly listening guests into gales of laughter.

But in the midst of the infectious fun, Miss Marsh, suddenly roused to a sense of her responsibilities, sprang to her feet.

"Oh, I forgot! Why, we're having a party, and we've all got to go back to it right this minute. And you haven't even been intro- duced, have you? Well, never mind, come on. Let's all go back and finish the party," and she held out an inviting hand.

"I love parties—always did, you know," sighed the lady of the mobcap; "but I've lost my fan and gloves."

"Let's go find them. Never mind if we are late." Seizing each other by the hand and laughing harder than ever, this very aston-ishing pair set out forthwith in hot pursuit of the party, in their haste forgetting all about the fan and gloves.

The sheep, of course, followed, as it is in the nature of sheep to do. Arrived at the party, Miss Marsh sent Bee out into the kitchen after her mother; and the instant she appeared, hot and flurried, the lady of the mobcap cried out in sudden joy, "Why, Sue Hoit! And so you married Dave Marsh after all, didn't you? And how you did keep him guessing, dear old Daisy!"

But Mrs. Marsh continued to stare in a puzzled sort of way at the laughing lady in the quaint mobcap. "I don't—seem—to place you," she said uncertainly.

"Aunt Polly!" prompted Cousin Marcella insinuatingly, "a tub of doughnuts—you surely remember that tub of doughnuts—and the Thanksgiving party—and a girl singing up at big, tow-headed Joe Grubb, otherwise 'Josie Cottontop,' just like this—'O cruel, cruel Tommy Tompkins!'"

"Oh, could I ever forget?" and Mrs. Marsh burst into a peal of laughter, and seizing the mysterious lady in the mobcap, cried, "Is it possible that you are Ba-a—"

"Sh-sh!" warned Cousin Marcella. "She doesn't want anybody to know yet. Isn't that just like her—hiding her light under a bushel, here in the old town, too?"

Bee Marsh could stand it no longer.

"Mother," she implored, her eyes wide with wonder, "who *is* she?"

"Oh, she was a girl who descended, bag and baggage, one wonderful day on the old Havenhill Academy, and we never knew a dull hour afterward, did we, Marcella? Her name in those days was—"

"Sh-sh!" and taking up the narrative, Cousin Marcella

continued: "She stayed with us through four golden years, and then she went away. Finally she married, and you know that's the way all proper story books end."

"But I know this one doesn't end that way," persisted Bee; but nobody paid the least attention to her, for the three old schoolmates were started again, and this time it was of a stirring-off at a camp in the woods they talked. "Did you ever taste anything half so good, and did you ever have so royal a time even at Buckingham Palace?" suddenly asked Cousin Marcella of the lady in the mobcap.

"No, I never did," was the candid admission; "but then, they never, to my knowledge, had a stirring-off there—at least, never when I was present."

Bee plucked her mother's sleeve violently. "What about Buckingham Palace?" she cried eagerly. "Has she ever been there?"

"Oh, many times!" It was Cousin Marcella answering. "You see, her husband was for years in the British diplomatic service—is still, for that matter, though just now, I believe, he is off somewhere on some sort of mission for the government. At least I read that in some paper. Is that how you happen to be back here in your Aunt Polly Steele's old place?" and she turned to the lady of the mobcap.

"Yes," and the lady of the mobcap looked very young and wistful just then. "Ever since Aunt Polly died and the dear little place fell to me, I have cherished a dream of coming back to see the crabapple trees in bloom and to be a little girl again. I wanted Carola to know and love the same simple joys that sweetened the wholesome life of those dear days with Aunt Polly—bless her! How she did love us all, even when she scolded us with such vigorous good will! Besides, I wanted time to—" She stopped abruptly.

"You may as well out with it," broke in Cousin Marcella. "Say! I'm going to tell!"

She glanced around at the circle of girls clustering close, their young, immature faces touched with a kind of awe compounded of wonder and wistfulness. They no longer looked to her like absurd fashion plates. They were only girls, just girls, pathetically eager to get the best out of life, and so woefully ignorant of what the best really is.

"My dears," and she stretched her arms out as though to take them all in, "wouldn't you like to know Barbara Anne Moffett?"

"Who writes all those books, those perfectly splendid books?" cried one and another, the excitement running high. "Oh! Oh! Oh!"

"Yes!" exclaimed Miss Marsh, "the very same. Here she is, writing cap and all. Barbara Anne Moffett, get up and make your bow."

"Oh, my biscuits!" suddenly and inopportunely wailed Mrs. Marsh, throwing up tragic hands. "I know they're burned to a crisp."

And they were. But nobody minded it, not even Bee, that stickler for ceremony and form. Amid much laughter everybody, imitating Miss Marsh's merry example, sallied out into the kitchen to seize trays and help themselves to whatever viands were in sight and quickly scurry back lest they miss some of the fun. It was the most informal party that can be imagined. But such talk! Such fine, flowing, luminous discourse as none there had ever listened to, or was ever likely to hear again. It was as if a magic curtain were being lifted on an infinitely wider and more gracious world than any girl there had ever dreamed of, as the

two gifted women, each spurring the other on, told of their trav-
els, of the notable men and women they had met here, there, and
everywhere, and rehearsed the rich and varied human experiences
that grow out of prolonged residence abroad.

"The biscuits burned up; nobody noticed the decorations; and
everything turned out differently from the way I'd planned it,"
said Bee to Cousin Marcella when the two found themselves
alone in the empty drawing-room, the last lingering guest having
gone reluctantly away; "but," she added in a burst of rapture,
"there never was such a party. The girls will never forget it,
never."

"Now, just why was it different from your other parties?" and
Miss Marsh turned penetrating eyes on Bee.

"Well, first of all it was the guests"; and Bee folded her hands
one over the other in a kind of wordless ecstasy. "It would have
been grandeur enough for one afternoon just to meet you,
Cousin Marcella, but when Barbara Anne Moffett—why she's so
splendid that it fairly took one's breath away!"

"Splendid, *Barbara Anne,* in that rig of hers?"

"Oh, what difference did it make what she had on?" cried Bee
impatiently. "Five minutes after seeing her you forgot everything
but that sparkling face of hers, and her talk just lifts you into a
kind of paradise. I can't say it, but, O Cousin Marcella, I feel it in
here." Bee laid her hand on her heart. "It's so silly and so utterly
hopeless, but," she added in a kind of shamefaced humility, "how
I long to be like her!"

"Yes, I know," came very gently from Cousin Marcella as she
drew the girl down beside her on the low lounge. "I felt that way
myself as a girl; we all felt that way. It has been the effect always
of Barbara Moffett's radiant personality; but while none of us ever
could be just like her, for God has given her certain rare gifts

denied the rest of us, we can each measurably approach her in the qualities which, more than her brilliancy, are the real basis of her enduring charm. Now, let me ask you one question: Which of all the girls here this afternoon did she apparently take the most pleasure in meeting?"

"She was nice to them all," Bee said after prolonged thought; "but—well, it did seem to me that she paid more attention to the Leary girl than to any of us."

"You are right. She did. Her keen insight told her that here was a girl definitely barred out of other girls' good times, and she wanted, somehow, to make it up to her. That was always Barbara Anne's way. I say her insight told her that. It may be, however," went on the steady, remorseless voice, "that she had intimate knowledge of it through Carola, who possibly suffered a like ostracism on account of—"

"Oh, don't—please *don't* remind me of what I said about their rag carpet," suddenly wailed Bee, seeing a great light. "I never knew before that I was such a snob, such a pitiful, contemptible snob," and a burst of hysterical tears accompanied the admission.

For some moments she wept on without restraint, Miss Marsh making no attempt either to console her or to check the flow of her tears. At length the storm passed; and a humbled, contrite, softened Beatta, with none of the cocksure arrogance of the old Beatta, lifted a wet, appealing face.

"I don't know what ever made me so—so horrid," she said between sobbing catches of breath; "but—but—I wanted so much to be somebody—to have folks look up to me—and all the girls want me in their crowd."

The foolish little confession was hardly out when Bee, as though to expose all the secrets of a scoured soul, hurried on: "Oh! I see it—I see it all now! I've gone after the wrong things, and gone after them in the wrong way. I've hurt others, but I've hurt myself worst of all; for I have been snippy to Carola just as I've been snippy to those other girls, and now—I've lost her for a friend, and—and I've lost Barbara Anne Moffett, too. But, O Cousin Marcella," she clutched despairingly after Miss Marsh, "you won't cast me off, will you?"

"Of course not, Beatta," said the wise Miss Marsh, perceiving that the lesson had gone home, "nor will anyone whose friendship is really worthwhile cast you off. You know, dear, it comes to us all at some time or another to look into Bobby Burns's mirror; but if, having once seen ourselves 'as ithers see us,' we strive with all the might that's in us to alter the reflection, nobody—least of all a Barbara Anne Moffett—is going to hold the past against us."

G.G. MANTON

TABLE SERVICE

Author Unknown

When the boss invited Sam Hatcher to eat with him, the young salesman was torn between fear and euphoria: Was he to be fired or was he to be promoted? Neither, he soon discovered. He was to learn a lesson—a lesson in salesmanship, yes, but more significantly, a lesson in friendship, from an immigrant waitress named Olga. "It is one of the most beautiful compensations of life that no man can sincerely try to be of help to another without being of help to himself."

am Hatcher was standing at the store window listlessly watching the passing crowd. He was one of the salesmen on the floor in The Circle, the city's largest furniture store. Sam found the monotony of his work and the lack of opportunity distasteful.

"How about going to lunch with me this noon, Sam?" The words startled him. Turning half around he was face to face with Tom Matthews, the store manager. "Can you make it?"

"Why yes—yes, of course," stammered Sam.

"All right, twelve-fifteen then," said the manager, leaving Sam excited, and wondering if this meant a promotion or dismissal. He hoped it would mean a transfer to the Contract Department, where not only would the pay be better but there'd be opportunities to get out in a car around the city on the trail of furnishing jobs in big apartments.

"Any special place you'd like to eat?" asked Matthews as they walked down the street. Sam shook his head. "Well, then, I'd like to take you to a restaurant I'm fond of. How were your sales this morning?"

Sam hesitated. "Nothing worth talking about. Just a newly married couple with two hundred hunting something for nothing, and an old lady looking for an easy chair. I sold her, but I bet she won't like it—one of the fussy kind that changes their mind every two minutes, you know."

Matthews nodded. "We get all kinds. How do you like your work?"

"Well, to be honest with you, I'd like it better in Contract. I put in an application there, but never heard from it. No opportunity on the floor—just selling odds and ends: nothing interesting about it, I mean. I'd like a chance to show what I can do."

Matthews nodded again.

"Well, here we are," he said, and the two men entered the noisy restaurant. The proprietor, Jules Wayne, lifted two beckoning fingers to the head waitress.

"I'd like one of Olga's tables, Jules," said Matthews.

"Oh—the brown-haired one. I'm sorry, Mr. Matthews; every one of her tables is full. Will you take another table or—"

"We'll wait," said Matthews.

Sam wondered, and Matthews smiled. "I always try to get this particular waitress. The only trouble is, so do about fifty others. And it's not because of her looks," he added, chuckling at Sam's wide smile. "She's a plain little tike but I've known busy men to wait ten minutes to get one of her tables."

They waited five minutes, and then a table for two was vacated in Olga's section. Sam took a look. She was plain-featured, almost homely, but the smile and greeting she gave them were so charming, Sam forgot all else.

"You bring a friend, Mr. Matthews?" she said, smiling warmly. Sam noticed she spoke with a strong accent—Russian or Polish, he decided. But that handicap also vanished, as she said, "I would like to know your friend's name," with disconcerting frankness.

Matthews chuckled. "Sam Hatcher, Olga. He works at The Circle, too."

"Oh, you work in that nice store." The waitress beamed. "That is fine. But you work hard—you are hungry. The plate lunch is good. You like corned beef and cabbage, Mr. Hatcher?"

"I'm crazy about it," grinned Sam, submitting to her friendliness to a degree that amazed him inwardly. Olga took the orders briskly, and hurried away, shaking her finger on route at a young man at the next table. "You eat too fast," she admonished. "You promised me not to."

The young man laughed, and catching Matthews' eye upon

him, said, "Some gal, isn't she? She thinks I'm ruining my health because I eat my lunch too quickly."

Matthews laughed. So did several others around them. Somehow there was an air of friendliness and cheer and understanding pervading this section of the big restaurant. "That waitress," said Matthews, leaning across the table to Sam, "just runs the diet of everybody here, and makes them like it. Notice that old chap over there eating liver and spinach? He's anemic, and she makes him eat that three times a week. He pretends to get angry about it, but he loves being bossed around by her. It isn't impudence; she really *is* interested in every customer. Notice how she wanted to know your name right away? She knows them all. And if you think she won't remember that you liked corned beef and cabbage—just come here next time they have it on the plate lunch and see!"

Their lunch was before them, smoking hot, in no time. Olga brought their coffee, then darted to another table. In a few minutes she was back, hovering like an anxious hostess over their table. "Is it good? You like that corned beef, Mr. Hatcher?"

"Great!" replied Sam. Somehow it tasted better than corned beef and cabbage had ever tasted in a restaurant before. Olga clasped her hands and smiled delightfully. "Oh, I'm glad. Then you come back again."

"Yes—I'll come back again," grinned Sam; and he meant it, too.

As the two men left the restaurant, Matthews halted to speak to Jules. "That brown-haired waitress of yours is a smart one, Jules."

The proprietor looked around cautiously. "Listen, Mr. Matthews, she packs the house. I'm scared somebody will hire her away from me. I give her a bonus—and her tips! You should see them! Believe me, she makes plenty. Ten months ago she came over in the steerage—didn't even know the language. Think of it!"

On the way back to the store Sam was very quiet. He had a pretty good idea of Matthews' purpose in taking him to lunch— to see Olga in action; to see what enthusiasm could do to change a dreary job into a joy.

Back on the floor, Sam thought again of the newlyweds. He had been a little indifferent when he found they wanted to furnish a whole house with two hundred dollars. How would Olga have handled them? Sam grinned a little guiltily. Perhaps Olga would have been all excited about the thought of newlyweds furnishing their first home. Perhaps she would have planned and worked with the credit man to see if they couldn't make the two hundred stretch a long way. Perhaps she would have sold them, and made them such friends of the store that every stick of furniture the newlyweds should buy from then to their golden wedding would come from The Circle.

And the old lady—instead of being bored, as he was, perhaps Olga would have clasped her hands in ecstasy and exclaimed, "Oh, an easy chair you want—for yourself to sit in? Soft— cozy—so nice it must be for sewing and reading, and taking a nap in! I have a chair you go—what you say—crazy about! Let me show you." And she would have sold the chair—to stay sold. And the old lady would think The Circle the finest store on earth.

━━━━━◆━━━━━

Six months later, Tom Matthews took Sam to lunch at Jules' again. Over the coffee cup he offered Sam the coveted job in Contract, and there was the hint of an amused smile behind his shrewd eyes as he said, "You've developed marvelously in the last six months, Sam! They tell me you have more people asking for you than any other salesman in the house. Contract needs a man with your enthusiasm and interest in customers."

Sam smiled. "But, honestly, Mr. Matthews, I hate to leave the floor job—it's been—"

Olga hastened up to the table. "I warm up the coffee for you—yes?"

Sam rose and gravely extended his hand to the brown-haired waitress. "Olga, I want to thank you for getting me a promotion."

Olga took Sam's hand. *"Me?* I get you a better job? I don't know how—but I'm so glad for you. You will be success-ful—will he not, Mr. Matthews?"

Tom Matthews looked up at Olga and smiled. "I don't see how anything can stop him."

WHEN MUDDY CREEK
OVERFLOWED

Harriet Lummis Smith

*S*ome people have everything: looks, charm, brains, and wealth. Others are shortchanged all along the line. Anne Temple had it all and was considered a shoo-in for the coveted Jane Dillon medal. But all that was before the big farmer girl, Cornelia Rudd, entered the class. Cornelia lacked everything Anne had—except brains. And she had desperately set her sights on that medal.

And so the battle was joined . . . and a muddy creek would determine the outcome—or should have. Along the way, both girls learned the true meaning of friendship.

n exciting contest was going on in the Marburg Academy. Not only the students but the townspeople as well were watching with interest, taking sides, and freely prophesying the outcome. The Jane Dillon medal, awarded to the girl student who got the highest marks during her senior year, was not an empty honor; it meant a scholarship at Eaton College.

Everyone in school had taken for granted that when Anne Temple reached her senior year she would have everything her own way, just as she had had ever since her kindergarten days. Anne's fairy godmother who had endowed her with good looks, family prestige, and charm, had not failed to add brains. Anne learned rapidly, remembered accurately, and led her class apparently without exerting herself or sacrificing any of her pleasures.

Then at the beginning of Anne's senior year, Cornelia Rudd had entered the class. Cornelia was a big, raw-boned silent girl, the daughter of a farmer who had just recently rented a farm lying to the west of Marburg. It had taken a week for the school to realize that at last Anne had a rival. Anne herself had recognized it the first day.

"That Rudd girl isn't much to look at," Kitty Merrill remarked to Anne, "but she's as smart as lightning, just the same."

Anne admitted it without argument.

"Of course I never pretended to have any brains," continued Kitty, whose right to the title of class dunce was unquestioned, "but if I wanted the Jane Dillon medal, I'd keep an eye on Cornelia Rudd."

Cornelia had one tremendous advantage over Anne. Her school work was everything to her. She did not care for any of the outside interests that meant so much to Anne. She had never been to a party in her life, and had not the slightest desire to go to one. She took no part in the social life of the school, in which Anne was the leader, as she was the leader in its intellectual life. Cornelia might have claimed as her motto the saying, "This is the thing that I was born to do." Study was her recreation as well as her work. Anne was not the first to discover that the rival with the single aim is the rival to be dreaded.

The year went on. Anne studied harder than ever, and stopped going out so many evenings in the week; Cornelia held steadily to her course. Cornelia had a double incentive: she wanted to win partly because she suspected that her schoolmates were all on Anne's side, but principally because, unless she won the scholarship, her education was likely to stop with the Academy. When Cornelia thought of that, her face wore an expression of determination that would have made Anne apprehensive had she seen it.

By midwinter most of their classmates thought that Cornelia would come out ahead, though all acknowledged that the race was close. A trifle might throw the victory to either of the rivals. Anne was beginning to look a little wan, and her young friends remonstrated. What was the use of killing herself? It wasn't worthwhile to win the medal if it meant giving up all the fun of her senior year. To such remonstrances Anne invariably replied, "I may be beaten—sometimes I think I'm going to be—but it won't be because I didn't try."

All winter long Cornelia had walked to and from school— three miles every morning and three miles back in the afternoon. She had faced many a storm, and several times had waded through unbroken snowdrifts, but she had never come so near losing her courage as when on one of the days that are neither spring nor winter but that have all the bad qualities of both, she came upon what looked like a lake across the familiar road.

Muddy Creek, ordinarily an insignificant little stream showing now on one side of the road and then on the other, had received such accessions from the melting snow and the spring rains that it was no longer recognizable.

Cornelia stood staring at the sheet of water that barred her way. The wind ruffled its surface exactly as if it had been a real lake, leaving in her mind the impression that the water was laughing at her. Cornelia never wasted words. "Well!" she said—and stopped with that, though her tone implied that it was anything but well. Apparently the sensible course was to turn back, especially as she was likely to find the road under water at several places farther along. But being absent from school just now was a serious matter. Cornelia was as well aware as anyone that she and Anne were very close.

"I won't go back!" she exclaimed as vehemently as though somebody had been urging her to do it. "I won't." She stared defiantly at the water and then began to take off her storm galoshes, her stout shoes, and her woolen stockings.

The middle of March is not the season for going barefooted. Cornelia gasped as she put her foot down on the muddy road, and with each step she gasped again. It took four steps to bring her to the water. Although it was no time to stand deliberating, she hesitated. But after realizing that she did not intend to go back, it was necessary for her to go forward. Then she thought of Anne, and hesitated a little longer. Gathering her skirts about her, she stepped resolutely into the icy water. The shock of it surprised her and she uttered a muffled shriek, yet she went splashing ahead until she presently found herself on dry ground; her legs and feet ached agonizingly, and her teeth chattered. She set herself to start the circulation by vigorous rubbing, and then put her shoes and stockings on again.

I suppose this is just a waste of time, she said to herself gloomily. *They'll have to come off again.*

As a matter of fact they did come off again, not once, but twice. Cornelia did no more shrieking. She went ahead with a curious feeling of desperation, as if she were to go on forever, floundering through pools as cold as ice. When at last the road to town branched off and left Muddy Creek to its own devices, she felt unreasonably certain that, if she had come to one more spot where the road was overflowed, she would have sat down by the water's edge and cried.

It was fortunate that Cornelia always started for school early. In spite of the delay she arrived ten minutes before the hour of opening. She felt damp and chilled and exhausted. Yet she did not present herself as a conquering heroine. Moreover, she had dropped one of her books into the water, and though she had saved it, its appearance caused her keen anguish. Her regard for books made her almost as uncomfortable over mistreating them as she would have felt at seeing an animal abused.

Kitty was in the cloakroom when Cornelia entered, and her blue eyes bulged at sight of her. "Why, Cornelia Rudd!" she cried shrilly. "How did you get here?"

"Walked," answered Cornelia.

"Yes, I know, but—why, our milkman couldn't get through this morning! He telephoned and said that the water was all over the road."

The girls crowded around. Cornelia found herself a little impatient of their interest and yet a little flattered by it, too. "Of course, the water's over the road," she replied shortly. "But it's not deep as a well."

"Isn't it over your galoshes?"

"Galoshes!" Cornelia did not often laugh, but the question

moved her to merriment. "Well, rather," she said at last. "I suppose it was a little over two feet deep in the deepest parts. Your milkman must be more afraid of water than most of 'em are," she added witheringly.

The girls laughed admiringly at the sally, but Kitty, who when a question puzzled her had a striking way of sticking to it till she understood it, stared incredulously at Cornelia's feet. "I should think you'd be sopping wet!" she exclaimed.

"Oh, I took off my shoes and stockings and waded."

There was a shriek of blended horror and amazement.

Looking about, Cornelia saw that the faces gazing at her were full of friendly admiration. She tried to persuade herself that it made no difference to her, but human nature is human nature, and the girl was never yet born who could be entirely indifferent either to friendliness or to admiration. Then at the back of the room Cornelia caught sight of Anne, gazing at her with an expression that she did not altogether understand. Cornelia picked up her books and moved away.

At ten o'clock the Virgil class filed into the room of the Latin teacher, Miss Train. Cornelia was the second one who was called on to recite. They were reading the sixth book; she loved the flowing syllables of the old-time poet. Gallantly struggling to make her translation not unworthy of the original, she began in an unusually husky voice:

"Night rushes on, Aeneas. We are protracting the hours with weeping. Here is a spot where the road divides in two directions, the right which leads—"

Cornelia stopped short, realizing that she was going to sneeze. As the class sat waiting for her to do so, smiles appeared on the faces turned in her direction. There is indeed something ridiculous about a sneeze. A cough has a tragic import. No one ever thinks of laughing at a cough. But a sneeze, with its bluster of preparation and the following explosion, appeals to everyone's sense of humor.

Cornelia sneezed three times while her classmates waited smilingly, and then she took a breath—and went on sneezing. At the sixth explosion irrepressible giggles broke out all over the room. But Cornelia did not stop with six sneezes. She went on to nine, and when at last she finished, the room was in an uproar. Even Miss Train laughed.

Cornelia, hot and shaken, and her eyes swimming with tears, waited for the tumult to subside.

Miss Train hastened quiet by rapping for order. "I think we must excuse you from anything more today, Cornelia," she said kindly. "And after school, my dear, do take something for that cold!"

In the back of the room one girl had not laughed, but had sat looking at Cornelia's convulsive struggles with grave sympathy. Kitty had explained to her how Cornelia had reached school that day: "Water all over the road, you know. Our milkman couldn't get across, and that girl took off her shoes and stockings and waded through. What do you think of that?"

"H'm!" Anne had said noncommittally.

The Virgil recitation was half done when a dash of rain struck the windowpane. Cornelia looked up with a start. The sky was overcast again. The rain was beginning anew. And as she stared out at the wet path she felt the bitterness of defeat. She was beaten, and she knew it. She could probably wade back as she had waded over that morning, though every drop of rain made matters worse, but she could not continue to do it. As it was, she had taken a serious risk. She would have to stay home till the swollen creek had subsided, and even if she studied as hard as she could, she would miss innumerable little aids by which Anne would profit. It needed only a trifle to tip the scales. Those rain-drops beating maliciously against the glass of the window were enough.

Cornelia had never given much thought to Anne as a girl. Anne had been only an obstacle in the way of realizing her ambi-tion. Now, for the first time, she felt hostility toward her. It wasn't fair! Some girls had everything without trying. Now even the weather had taken sides with Anne!

The rain increased as the hours went on. Cornelia dragged from class to class, the victim of unconquerable depression. The road home was likely to be under water for half a mile or more. She would be lucky if she did not become deathly ill after two such wettings in a day. And once home, sick or well, she was imprisoned there till the water went down. Even in the time of the year when there was the least to be done on the Rudd farm, to spare one of the horses to take the only daughter to school was out of the question. Cornelia had discovered the fact so long before that she now simply accepted it. She was beaten.

In the half hour's intermission allowed for luncheon, Cornelia sat at her desk and did not eat. Several girls came up to inquire about her cold, and one brought her some small chocolate-coated pills, which she assured her would break a cold if taken in time. Cornelia immediately swallowed two as directed. She had reached the point where nothing seemed to matter.

When school was dismissed, she remained at her desk. She made her school books into piles, one for each arm. It would be necessary to take them all home so as not to get behind in her classes. Someone came up and stood beside her. Turning her head, she saw Anne. For all the day was so dark, there was a curi-ous light on Anne's face.

"Cornelia," she said, "I don't see how you can get home, with the creek rising all the time."

"I'm like the woodchuck that climbed the tree," said Cornelia. "He did it because he had to, and it's the same with me."

"And if you get home, I don't see how you're going to get back."

Cornelia made a little impatient movement. To herself she angrily retorted that it wasn't necessary for Anne to *rub it in*. But her answer, spoken dryly, was: "No, I don't see either."

"I was thinking," Anne went on talking rather fast, "that if you could telephone your mother, so she wouldn't be frightened, you could come home with me and stay until the roads are better."

Cornelia stared at her. For a bright girl she had considerable difficulty in understanding a simple English sentence. "Do you mean—," she began and found herself unable to go farther.

"It would be a shame for you to miss any of school just now," said Anne. "I'd be ever so glad to have you stay with me. You can telephone your mother, so she won't worry, and I can let you have the things you'll need."

Cornelia understood! The victory had been in Anne's hands, but she wanted it only if she could win it fairly. All at once Cornelia's heart was singing.

"We haven't a telephone," she answered, "but some neighbors of ours have, and they'll send word by somebody passing."

"Then we'll go home right away. You can use our telephone."

For more than a week Cornelia was a guest in the Temple home. Evening after evening she shut herself into a room, the luxury of which was almost distracting, and studied till midnight; and in a similar room across the hall Anne was equally industrious.

One of Anne's cousins, on learning the reason for Cornelia's presence in the house, had exclaimed sympathetically, "Why, if the poor thing wants it so much, why don't you just let her have it?"

Anne laughed. "You don't know Cornelia. If she wins, she wants to win in a fair race, just as I do."

At the end of ten days Muddy Creek was again on its good behavior, and Cornelia resumed her six-mile walk a day. Her stay at Anne's had been a tremendous advantage. The time it took to get to and from school and the other hours she gave to helping with the household tasks had all been devoted to study. *"If I win,"* she said to herself, *"it'll be Anne's doings."*

The examinations came as usual in the hottest days of June, but two girls of Marburg Academy went through them oblivious of the temperature. Then one breathless night the town's so-called "Opera House"—though no opera had ever been given in it—was crammed to suffocation with the friends and relatives of the graduating class. A distinguished visiting speaker paid compliments and offered good advice, and then the mayor, looking unhappy, gave a little more advice and distributed the diplomas. Last of all came the thing for which a good many people in the audience were waiting: the announcement of the prizes.

"The Jane Dillon medal, carrying a scholarship at Eaton College, is awarded to Miss Cornelia Rudd."

Cornelia's face was a chalky white. *Anne's lost it,* she said to herself.

But Anne, joining in the applause that swept through the hall, was pleasantly surprised to discover that she felt no disappointment. *Dear old Cornelia,* she felt herself thinking. *It would have been cruel if she hadn't won, when it meant so much for her to win.*

When the two girls got a chance for a word, it was Anne who was radiant. "Cornelia, I'm glad, I honestly am!"

"It was all your doings," Cornelia said with tremulous lips.

And then she realized that the best thing that she had won in that year in the Marburg Academy was not the diploma clutched in her warm hand or the coveted medal and all that it implied, but Anne herself. Out of that generous rivalry had grown a friendship that would permanently enrich the lives of both. As Cornelia went out into the night it seemed to her that, like the June sky, the future was spangled with stars.

Harriet Lummis Smith
(d. 1947)

authored the Peggy Raymond series for girls (written 1913–1922), but is perhaps best known for continuing the Pollyanna series begun by Eleanor Porter.

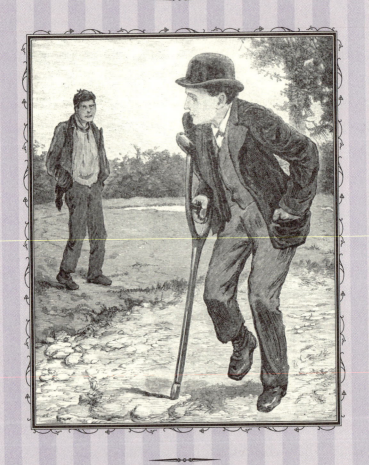

FRAMEWORK

Josephine De Ford Terrill

*C*harles, as leader of the gang, had just excluded
Humpy, the new boy in town, from both their friendship
and their baseball team: "I don't think a hunchback
ought to expect to be on a team."

His father, overhearing him, said nothing . . . but he
felt it was time. . . .

he "gang" was noisily chatting its way home from the baseball diamond, where the newly chosen Harper team had just completed its first afternoon of practice. Charles Hanford, the leader of the gang, stopped abruptly on the sidewalk, and the three boys shuffling along with him skidded to a respectful halt beside him.

"Well, why argue anymore about it?" he demanded. "We know how we are going to choose. We have nothing against Humpy. He's OK. But our team has got to have dignity. What will Waverly and Mayview think of us having a hunchback for our ump?"

"Yeah!" chorused the boys in disgruntled harmony.

Charles slapped his catcher's mitt resoundingly against one corduroy hip, and drew his blond brows together in fifteen-year-old seriousness. "You see, fellows, the ump is a mighty important part of a team. And people won't think we are much of a team if we have to depend on a cripple to tell us what is right and what isn't."

"Sure, they won't."

Charles resumed his way down the street, the boys falling again into step with him. "Of course, we must admit Hump is good. He knows his stuff. And of course it isn't his fault he's a cripple. But to tell you the truth, fellows," and here he lowered his voice impressively, "I don't think a hunchback ought to *expect* to be on a team."

It took the boys a moment to digest the significance of this thought. Then Bud agreed with conviction. "That's right. He oughtn't." Fred felt the same way now that the thought had been suggested to him.

The boys moved on until they came to the large dry goods store owned by Charles's father. Mr. Hanford was just leaving for the day, and he stood listening to the boys as they continued their discussion.

"Hump's good at books, but he isn't an athlete," stated Fred.

"Wonder why Professor Griggs doesn't tell him to stay out of games," suggested Bill.

"Well," drawled Charles lazily, conscious of his father's presence, "a teacher's got to be impartial. They have to have a lot of sympathy for unlucky guys like Hump." And with a farewell swing of the hand, he dismissed the boys and turned to his parent.

———⟶•⟵———

A few weeks later Charles was overjoyed by the news that his father's brother was coming to visit them for a month. Uncle Ben lived in an Eastern city, and wrote a column in the newspaper called "Better Than Blarney." Grandmother often sent them clippings of the column, and Father was very proud of them. Charles had never seen his uncle, but he had heard much of him, and felt that he must be a very great and important man.

As the train drew into the little town, the boy detached himself from the gang, whom he had invited to the station to meet his famous relative, and stepped up beside his father on the platform. His excitement was mixed with awe as he watched a tall, well-dressed man coming down the train steps behind the brakeman. But Charles slumped aghast when his father sprang forward and grasped the hands of a shriveled little man in gray, who had followed next. In horror Charles took in the diminutive figure with a pronounced upward bulge between the shoulders. A *hunchback!* The blood surged into his face and then slowly drained away, leaving it cold and drawn. Surely this could not be his uncle! But his father's long and affectionate greeting left no doubt in his mind. His eagerness crumpled into little pieces as he adjusted himself to the swift and agonizing disappointment. By the time the men were ready to turn to him, he had recovered somewhat and was able to meet the large gray eyes that looked up into his. Something in their twinkling depths helped him to steady his own. He found himself lost in them, fascinated, unconscious for a moment of anything else. There was no beginning nor end to them, no bounds, only a deep clearness set with bits of fire. Never before had Charles been so held by a pair of eyes. Only when a quick smile half veiled them, did he feel himself again, and heard a warm, deep voice saying, "And so this is the great big son!"

Taking one of the large suitcases, Charles followed his father to the automobile. He scarcely saw the boys as they stood in a huddle by the station door, staring in united astonishment. The desire to introduce his uncle to them was gone. A strange feeling of disgrace bore heavily down upon him as they drove away.

At home it was left to Charles's mother and Uncle Ben to carry on the conversation. Charles went about silent and crestfallen, and Father seemed dulled by a strange melancholy. Charles wondered for a moment if he also were ashamed of the small, stooped figure, but when he saw the tenderness in his eyes, he knew that it was an overwhelming pride that his father felt for his brother.

At bedtime Mother went upstairs to see that the guest room was in readiness, and Father found a chore to do outside. Uncle Ben crossed the room and sat down beside Charles on the lounge, and laid a hand upon his knee.

"Well, my boy," he said, "I am sorry you were so cruelly disappointed in your uncle tonight."

Charles flushed hotly. He opened his lips to make a shamed denial, but his uncle stopped him with a shake of the head. "I am used to reading faces, Charles. And I am also used to seeing that look of disappointment on the faces of people who have never seen me before. But it doesn't hurt me anymore. There used to be a sore place in my heart fully as large as the hump on my back, but though the hump remained, the pain in my heart gradually went away. And I don't believe anything could hurt me now unless it might be that my strong and splendid young nephew should never forgive me for being a hunchback."

For all of Charles's tall length and sturdiness, he was not many years removed from his small-boy days, and now, as in those days, he found refuge in a burst of tears. Why he cried he did not know—whether from pity or in sudden admiration, or whether from disappointment over his own crushed hopes. But his pent-up feeling found relief. He clasped his uncle's hand and held it.

Uncle Ben went on. "It was pretty hard growing up, or rather, not growing up. Young fellows don't always understand the feelings of unlucky chaps like me. Your father fought my battles for many years. It seemed that the gibes of our playmates hurt him almost more than they did me."

While he paused, ruminatively, Charles managed to say: "I am so ashamed, Uncle Ben."

"I understand," responded his uncle quickly. "And I meant it when I told you I was sorry to be a disappointment to you. Your father told me how eager you were over my coming. But he thought it best, for reasons of his own, not to tell you of my affliction."

Charles looked up wonderingly, but Uncle Ben resumed. "I hope that we can be friends in spite of it, Charles. I have lots of young friends in our block at home. I made up my mind years ago that I wouldn't let the shape of my body determine the shape of my life. My framework is badly out of line, but I refuse to let it make me grotesque and small inside. Fortunately, we have no bones in our hearts to become twisted and broken."

Mother appeared in the doorway. Uncle Ben arose and said smilingly, "Well, I'll see you in the morning."

It was a long time for a healthy boy to lie awake, but Charles did not sleep until he had thought it all out. All evening he had been wondering how he could face the boys in the morning. He had bragged so much about his uncle; had hunted up the clippings of the newspaper column, and read them to his friends, pretending to understand the full meaning underlying the crisp sentences. Now, with burning mortification, he recalled how heartless had been his attitude toward the little hunchback who had moved to their town last fall. He had never deliberately hurt or taunted him, but had just taken it for granted that Humpy and he lived in different worlds. That Humpy might be bitterly dissatisfied with his world had never occurred to him. *What a difference it makes when you have a cripple in your own family,* thought Charles. *How well you understand!*

With these new thoughts in his heart, the boy felt almost eager for morning to come, so that he might go out and face his friends with a challenge in his eyes. He would show the boys that he was proud of his Uncle Ben, just as he had known he would be! And maybe he could even yet get Humpy put on the baseball team as umpire. His framework might be badly out of line, but he knew all the rules of baseball. He'd make a dandy ump.

And he did!

Josephine De Ford Jerrill

early in the twentieth century, wrote prolifically for America's inspirational magazines. Her voice deserves to be heard again.

SILAS PETERMAN'S INVESTMENT

Susan Huffner Martin

S*he was a little bedraggled girl who had walked eight miles barefoot, carrying a pail of blackberries that she intended as a present for a rich man she had never seen, a man she hoped would consider being her friend.*

And now the maid wouldn't even let her in!

The little girl in the faded dress trudged determinedly down the road. In one hand she carried a pail of blackberries; with the other she twisted and untwisted a string of her pink sunbonnet. She wore no shoes or stockings, but under the pink sunbonnet a pair of steady blue eyes looked out upon the world, undaunted by many hardships. Myrtilla Lucy was not a stranger to them.

All at once she stopped, set down her pail of berries, and looked away in the direction of a large, gray stone building that stood out against the sky on a distant hilltop. Her blue eyes gleamed, her lips parted in a smile, revealing even rows of teeth as white as seed pearls. She drew a long breath.

"It looks good, that school does," she whispered. "Oh, if I could only go there and learn things; I'm praying, praying that I can."

She stood there a moment longer gazing at the big stone building gilded by the splendor of a summer's sun. Then she picked up her pail of berries and walked on. Once more she stopped; this time to examine a stone bruise on her foot, but she was soon trudging bravely on again in spite of pain and weariness. She came at last into the town, with its beautiful residences, its wide streets, its well-kept lawns. At the largest and most imposing of these residences she stopped, climbed the stone steps leading to the broad, graveled walk, marched up to the large porch, and knocked at the massive door without touching the electric bell so near it.

A moment later, a white-capped maid opened the door. When she saw the barefooted little girl in the faded dress, she frowned.

"If you have anything to sell, you should go around to the back door," she said sharply. "No one but callers come here."

The little girl pushed back the sunbonnet from her forehead.

"I ain't got anything to sell, and I'm a caller, too," she answered with a certain childish dignity. "I've come to see Mr. Peterman."

The maid started.

"Law, child," she cried, "you ain't got no kind of a chance to see Mr. Peterman. He's the busiest man in town. He hasn't time to spend on little girls like you."

The child's eyes suddenly filled with tears. "But I've walked eight miles," she said, resolutely winking back the tears. "I've brought him these blackberries, too, and I must see him. I can't—" her lips set themselves in firm and sudden lines—"I can't go home until I do see him."

The maid looked at her again, at the weary little figure; the bare, dusty, small feet; the determined gleam of the blue eyes.

"Well, wait a minute," she said not unkindly, "and I'll see what Mr. Peterman says."

A moment later she came out.

"You can come in," she announced briefly. The little girl followed the maid through a wide and spacious hall into another room, where a man sat busy with some papers at a table. He had gray hair, sharp, shrewd eyes, and strong, rugged features. There was a stern, sad look on his face, as if he seldom smiled. He lifted his head when the two came in. The maid spoke.

"This is the little girl, Mr. Peterman."

Silas Peterman pushed away his papers.

"Well," he said, as the maid turned away, "what is it you want with me?"

The little girl came nearer. "May I sit down, sir?" she asked in a sweet, clear voice. "You see, I've walked a long way, and once I bruised my foot on a stone in the road."

"What did you take such a long walk for?" he demanded gruffly. "There, sit down, then."

The little girl took the chair he indicated, still keeping the pail of berries by her side.

"I wanted to see you," she said simply.

"To see me? What for?"

The little girl looked back at him gravely.

"I wanted to ask you," she began slowly, "if you wouldn't send me to that school for girls on the hill yonder. Folks tell me you've got heaps of money, and I thought maybe, when I explain things to you, you wouldn't mind having me for an investment."

"An investment?" cried Silas Peterman.

The little girl nodded.

"Yes, an investment. You see, sir, I've always wanted to learn, but at home I haven't any chance. Mother has five others besides me; and Dad, he can't do much, 'count of his poor health. I thought if I could get you to send me to school, why, when I did get educated, maybe I could do something for you. I ain't got no kind of a chance the way things are, so I picked these berries and brought 'em to you for a little present, and I made up my mind I'd come out open and honest and ask you to send me to that school. Nobody knows I come, not even Mother."

Silas Peterman stared at the small, shabby figure, too astonished to speak.

"What has made you come to me?" he demanded after a short silence.

The little girl sighed.

"There wasn't anyone else to come to," she replied. "I don't know of anyone that's got any money except you. I heard Dad tell Mother how rich you were, and you never put any money into anything that wasn't a good investment. And then, I thought I'd come and tell you that I'd be a good investment myself. I'm little now, but I'll grow, and maybe when I'm grown you'll be glad you helped me. You never can tell what will happen in this world. Oh, sir, please send me to school and let me learn. I'll pay it back, truly I will.

When you get old, I'll come and take care of you if you need anyone; but please, please send me to school. The world is just full of
things I don't know about. *To go without an education is most as bad as
being blind!* When you don't know anything, you can't see with your
mind. It's all dark. You understand what I mean, don't you?"

Silas Peterman continued to study the small, earnest face.

"That's a new thought," he answered, "about the mind being
blind if one isn't educated. And so," he added reflectively, "you
came to me to ask for help, and you brought me some blackberries in that pail, did you?"

"Yes, sir, the finest I could pick. It was all I could do for you,
but I think you'll like 'em. They make good pies."

She lifted the pail of shining blackberries and placed it on the
library table. There was a long silence.

"Well," said Silas Peterman at last, "I am inclined to accept
you as an investment, much as I know I shall regret it. I've been
disappointed a great many times in those I've tried to help, but
I'm going to give you a chance. It rests on you whether you
make good or not."

The little girl in the faded dress sprang up.

"You won't be sorry," she cried. "I'll learn everything I can,
and some day I'll do things for you—"

<hr />

"Come along, Myrtilla Lucy, come along," called a man in a blue
shirt and overalls one September morning. "Say good-bye to Ma and
the children. It's time to go." She wore a clean gingham dress, and
this time she had on shoes and stockings; but she still wore the pink
sunbonnet. A slender, stoop-shouldered woman in a limp calico
gown came out with her, followed by five little children.

"Good-bye, Ma," cried the little girl, flinging her arms about her mother's neck. "You won't miss me too much, will you? I'll be home Christmas, and I'll write you every week. Good-bye, Nellie and Luella and Bobby and Ned and Nancy. All of you help Mother."

"Good-bye, Myrtilla Lucy," they all cried in chorus. "Write us what they have to eat and if the teacher's cross or not."

"I will," said Myrtilla Lucy. "I will."

As they jogged along in the little rough wagon, her father turned to her. "It beats all that Silas Peterman is going to educate you," he said. "Folks do say that he's powerful close, and yet sending you to school don't look much like it. Well, I'm glad you are to have your chance, Myrtilla Lucy."

<hr />

"Well," said Mr. Silas Peterman to the president of the college one day, "how is that little girl I sent you last fall doing? Is there anything to her?"

The president of the college smiled. He was a portly gentleman, with kind eyes. "Yes, there is a great deal to her," he replied. "She's the brightest girl we have. She's at the head of all her classes. She leaves nothing unlearned that comes her way." He hesitated. "May I ask how it came that you decided to educate her?" he said.

"Well," replied Mr. Peterman, smiling at the memory of his protégée, "I'll tell you. I did it for an investment."

<hr />

It was twelve years later. The physician looked grave as he studied his patient.

"Mr. Peterman," he said finally, "you need a change, a trip, a long rest; but someone will have to go with you. Don't you know anyone—some capable young woman upon whom you could depend; someone who would keep things cheerful, and see to your meals and your medicine? Think, now; among all the young people you know surely there is someone."

Mr. Silas Peterman shook his head. He looked shrunken and old and sad as he sat there.

"Who wants to cheer up an old, crabbed invalid?" he replied. "What young person would be willing to devote her time to a sick man? I haven't anyone related to me to look after me, and I wouldn't ask it of her if I had. We'll say no more about it."

Just at that moment the door opened and a young lady entered. She was slender, erect, and blue-eyed—a very vision of health and hope and happiness.

"I've just heard of your illness, Mr. Peterman," she began, as she went forward to greet him. "I came on the first train."

Mr. Silas Peterman looked up. A smile broke all over the thin, worn face.

"If it isn't Myrtilla Lucy!" he said. "But what," he added, "have you done with your school?"

"They can get a substitute," she replied gayly; "but *you* can't—you know you can't. Nobody can take care of you as I can. I'm going to stay for as long as you need me. The school can take care of itself."

The physician's face immediately lost its anxious look.

"Just the thing," he cried approvingly. "And may I ask, sir," he added, turning to Silas Peterman, "who this young lady is?"

But it was Myrtilla Lucy who answered. She glanced down the vista of years and saw herself a small, ragged, barefooted girl, with her pail of blackberries in her hand. She saw the friend who had opened the magic doors of education to her and given her an entrance into that wider world. She owed everything to that sick, lonely old man in the invalid's chair opposite, and she did not forget it. Suddenly she bent forward and took Silas Peterman's hand, and pressed it lovingly between her two young, firm ones. Her turn had come. She looked at the physician.

"Did you not know," she said gayly, "that over twelve years ago Mr. Peterman made an investment? He took a little ragged girl out of a log cabin and sent her to college. I am that investment."

But it was Silas Peterman who spoke this time. He, too, looked down the long years, and saw Myrtilla Lucy as she had looked that August day, with her bare feet and faded dress, her eager blue eyes. She had told him then that some day he might need her. A great wave of thankfulness rolled over his heart. He wasn't alone any longer. After all, he had someone to lean on, someone who would stand in the place of his own daughter, had she lived. The little bare-footed girl in the faded dress had made good. He turned to his physician.

"Yes," he said, and his voice trembled, "she is an investment—and the best one I ever made!"

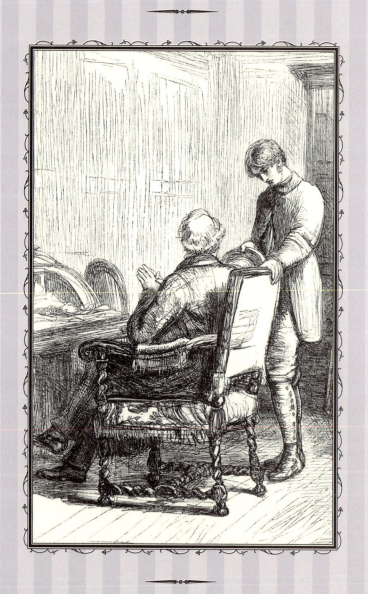

I CAN SEE HIM

Joseph Leininger Wheeler

I t always seemed to take forever—that slow walk from parking lot to office, or office to classroom. During the bad times, it would take even longer. During the worst times, he would not come in at all—only his voice would show up (in recordings) to speak to his classes. But the voice, divorced from the body language and slightly sardonic eyes, was a most inadequate substitute.

Strange, how clear it remains in my all-too-often fuzzy memory, forty-some years later. I may not be able to remember where I put my checkbook or a name I have known all my life, but the image and personality of this history professor remain as clear to me as what I see, hear, and experience today.

Like most college students, I was struggling for bedrock between two worlds: the world of my family and childhood and that rather frightening world of adulthood and responsibility. I was shy and insecure, doubting whatever gifts the Creator had entrusted to me. Oh, that was not my facade, which could veer between the brash and the naive, but that *was* the boy/man cowering behind that inconsistent front. My first role models, my parents, had completed (for better or worse) their job. Unbeknownst to me, I was now searching for a new guiding light, friend, inspiration, mentor, hero. I found all of these in Dr. Walter Utt, those many years ago.

It is said, "Show me your mentors, and I'll show you who you will some day be." I agree, in part. I say "in part" because mentoring that churns out mere clones is not real mentoring; *real* mentors are prospectors seeking gold in the vast accumulations of shale each of us houses within. Not transplanted gold, for that is mere watering of the mine, but the gold God buries somewhere in the strata of each child born on this planet. I point this out because all too often our mentors disregard the gold mine within us and sell us instead a bill of goods. Adulation is, after all, the headiest of wines, and rare is the man or woman who can steel the heart and mind against it. To switch metaphors: the natural tendency is for the mentor to fill the empty bottle of the mentoree with self, to create a clone. I have seen those mentored, years later, belatedly wake up to the sad realization that everything they felt was their own was in reality someone else's—their inner gold remained unsearched for and undiscovered. And they then hate that long-ago mentor for raping selfhood.

Were Dr. Utt that kind of mentor, I would not be bringing him back this warm spring day so many years later. He was as different as . . . well . . . as his lectures. And to really explain those, I'll need to take you time traveling—back to the 1950s.

I came to Pacific Union College in California's famed Napa Valley because—well, because my father had gone there and because his parents still lived nearby. Like most missionary kids, I came back to America out of sync. Socially and in sports I was an utter misfit. My sense of self-worth continued to erode. So did my up-till-then high grades. Failure—utter and complete failure—stared me in the face. And I hadn't the slightest inkling of how I could stave off disaster.

Enter Dr. Utt.

Oh, to be honest, I did have other mentors too: notably Professors Lewis Hartin and Paul Quimby—none of us has but one mentor. But, powerful as each of them was, compared to the drawing power of Dr. Utt's magnetic field, it was no contest.

Looking back at those rootless years, I ricocheted like a drunken bee, trying everything, sipping everything, floundering ever deeper into the morass of failure. I started out in theology because I came from a long line of ministers. But I felt no personal commitment to that calling. Greek came early, and my lackadaisical study habits and procrastination doomed me to failure there, where getting behind just one class greased your downward skid.

In my freshman year, the college unleashed upon its students a wild experiment: a two-year introduction to the world of ideas—literature, art, history, music, science, sociology, psychology, philosophy, and religion. Dr. Utt was one of the program's guiding gurus, and team-taught the humanities courses. I listened to him and was mesmerized. He and the program opened a door into a world I barely knew existed.

Some time later, I finally gathered together my shreds of courage and signed up for one of Dr. Utt's history classes. It was all that I had heard it would be—and more. Later I discovered that Dr. Utt never used the same set of notes twice. As history chair, adviser, and campus patron saint (term used advisedly), he was *always* surrounded by students, figuratively and sometimes literally sitting at his feet—listening and asking questions, a number content just to be near him, to bask in his presence. Perhaps because of his fragility (he was a hemophiliac and bled easily), we valued his wisdom all the more. Somehow, in the midst of all these interruptions, he managed to sketch out his class lecture in his inimitable hieroglyphics on whatever small piece of paper—often an envelope—was in range. By the time he painfully pushed out of the chair with the aid of his ever-present cane, he'd be ready for that next class.

We'd hear the shuffle of his shoes and the tap of his cane long before we'd see him. There in his classroom we'd be chuckling over the latest cartoons, usually from the *Saturday Evening Post*. His favorites had to do with world politics and history. But when he finally approached the desk, we'd open our tablets, grab a pen, and look up with an air of expectancy. Fools that we were, each time we'd vow that *this time,* it would be different. And each time it would be the same. Before very many moments had passed, we'd have lost all track of contemporary life and be immersed in another time. The past, to him, was always story—the story of unforgettable people. Those worlds became reality as Utt peopled them with flesh and blood. Words he wielded with all the finesse of a knight wielding a rapier of Toledo tempered steel. Profundities were camouflaged with wit and understatement: one moment, we'd be vainly trying to hold back tears, and another we'd be rolling in the aisles. Looking back, it seems akin to the unvarnished biographies in Scripture, complete with all the frailties, the full range of human thought and behavior. We felt we *knew* Utt's men and women; even in their mistakes of judgments, their tragedies, we *understood* why they acted as they did. And we felt part of the fabric of the age itself: given the stage upon which they lived, most likely we'd have been hard-pressed to do much better, be much wiser, than they. Out of all this came his supreme gift to us—tolerance.

Often we'd feel set up. Funniest, in retrospect, is to remember those who belatedly realized, all at once, a multitiered joke (complete with double, triple, and even quadruple entendres), and who convulsively rocked in a vain effort to bottle it up inside. Most often, they'd fail. In the uproar that ensued we'd sometimes catch the sardonic grin: *All that work not wasted after all—someone had caught it!*

Through it all, we never for a moment doubted Utt's basic empathy with the players brought back to life. Or that, no matter the hells set loose by the Dark Power, God remained at the helm. A kind, loving, forgiving, empathetic God—He alone capable of separating motive from act.

Then the bell would ring, the mists of another time would dissolve, the images blur, and contemporary time resume. We'd ruefully glance down at page after page of feverishly scrawled notes and know for certain that nothing after all was different: our words could not possibly recapture that magic of *being there* in the past. We'd compare notes and discover that even verbatim transcripts were lifeless without the visual reality of his presence. It was a compensatory gift from God, one of a kind. I've tried—oh, how I've tried!—to do the same, but failed every time. It was his gift alone. No other individual I have ever known has had the power to transport one into a three-dimensional Technicolor past, using mere words.

Those were halcyon days in the college on the hill. Parochial colleges were subject to the same ebb and flow, same ideological pendulum swings, experienced by society at large. It was, after all, the twilight of Norman Rockwell America: Family and Judeo-

Christian values were still paramount. Because of that societal serenity, liberals, centrists, and conservatives lived at peace with each other on our campus: there was almost perfect balance—I have never seen the like since. Powerful professors sparked our imagination and provided a vision for what we might someday become. The greatest Christian thinkers have invariably been well educated: Moses, Daniel, Paul, Augustine, Luther, to name just a few. For such titans, faith and intellect have blended seamlessly. From each of my professors, I learned and I grew. Some were pure otherworldly intellects, some were grand-standing prima donas, some were solid centrists, some were mav-ericks, some were Dostoyevskian Ivans (challenging everything), some were rockbound conservatives, preaching the true faith, and that only. And some, a precious Gideon's band, were Christian Renaissance men and women, embracing the entire philosophical spectrum—chief of these being Dr. Utt.

On Sabbaths we'd throng the rooms where the Great Ones—various learned professors—held forth. There was always a core lesson for a base, but it represented merely an ideological hockey puck: it might go *anywhere* once the invocation had been given. How their minds sizzled! How they delighted in giving spiritual and intellectual battle with each other! We students rarely dared to enter the lists; we'd have been pulverized in sec-onds. But we listened—oh how we listened! And, as we listened, as we assimilated, as we decided whom we agreed with and whom we disagreed with . . . we *grew*. And Dr. Utt was always, health permitting, in the center of the fray. By the twinkle in his eyes, we sensed his inner joy.

On Saturday evenings Dr. Elmer Herr, another history profes-sor, brought the world to our door in his Lyceum Series. It might be a symphony orchestra, it might be Arthur Rubinstein, it might be Fred Waring and his choir, it might be a drama, it might be a film—the best and the finest came to Irwin Hall, and it was unthinkable not to be there with your date.

Each history class I took from Utt did something to me, strengthened me. Eventually, I changed my majors to history and English. I got Dr. Utt to take me on as his reader, a role I cherished for three years, the last one as graduate assistant.

I can see him now in that long history office. Every once in a while I'd look up in response to his chuckle, as a particular *Saturday Evening Post* cartoon tickled his funny bone. His other obsessions, such as stamp collecting (especially from France and Monaco), military uniform prints, and anything having to do with the Reformation (especially Huguenots and Waldenses), gave zest to his days. And always there were my obnoxious classmates butting in and taking Dr. Utt's precious time. I was jealous, for I wanted all of him for myself. Some of these ever-present devotees at least expressed themselves intelligently, but there were others who gushed, fawned, and bored me and my fellow readers to death. What they said was so incredibly inane and naive. Surely Dr. Utt would put them in their place and tell them how monumentally stupid they were. But he *never* did. Never once during those years do I remember him putting anyone down or lowering anyone's feeling of self-worth. *He was invariably kind.* That was especially impressive to me as I had seen how thoroughly he could dispatch peer opponents in debate (no quarters were given in that arena).

In retrospect, I can see how much like Christ's disciples we were: attempting to drive out the children in order to have Christ all to themselves. Also, while in retrospect I can see Dr. Utt clearly; at that time I most definitely could not. Funny, isn't it, how the Creator programs us to flower gradually? Emily Dickinson put it this way:

> *Truth must dazzle gradually*
> *Or every man be blind.*

Well, the years passed, and eventually I had taken every class, undergraduate and graduate, Dr. Utt offered. Married then, I left to build on my own dreams. But it didn't take long for me to realize how tough the real world was. My first year's teaching came close to being my last. During that traumatic period, when it seemed my only logical alternative was to resign, my wife and I agonized and were never far from tears. Was this the end?

I'll never forget the early spring day we got into our car. Seemingly on its own volition, it took us west, west to the Napa Valley, then north to Angwin and the home of my mentor. We walked into an Utt family reunion, but they all welcomed us. Almost instantly, Dr. Utt read our faces: "Out with it, Joe; what's wrong?" I told him, and them. Late that afternoon we left, with stiffer backbones than we'd arrived with, and the Utt injunction, *Fight it out!* ringing in our heads all the way home. We did, and won. I stayed in teaching.

———◆———

The telephone rang in my office in Thousand Oaks, California, twenty-four years later. (For twenty-four years I had stayed in teaching. Then, feeling burned out, I had left teaching for full-time fund-raising.) I picked up the receiver and brightened momentarily—it was an old college friend. But I quickly sobered with his next words: *"Joe, Dr. Utt just died!"*

A part of me died that day.

Then my friend provided details. Dr. Utt had fallen and needed an immediate blood transfusion. The closest blood bank was in San Francisco. In those days, there were not the controls that there are today, and consequently the blood he received was contaminated with the AIDS virus. In Dr. Utt's weakened state, the end came quickly. There was to be a remembering service that coming weekend. Could I be there?

All during the trip north, I thought about Dr. Utt and his role in whatever I had been able to accomplish in life. I thought back to those years on campus when he had served as my bridge between adolescence and adulthood. But I thought even more about the years afterward, how he had somehow found time in his hectic schedule to stay in touch. His notes had been like all else that he laboriously scrawled: brief, pithy, cryptic, funny, and Utt-ish. As the darker days of the sixties and seventies had replaced the serene fifties, he'd sometimes note that the ideological climate had changed—"The brethren are at it again"—and I'd decode it to mean: *Some of the ultraconservatives perceive me as a liberal, and they are making it rather tough for me.* That was as close as he ever came to complaining. But since he always understated his problems, I knew by such an admission that things hadn't been easy for him in recent months. As for his physical ailments, not once did I ever hear him complain!

Those infrequent but cherished cards and short letters never failed to bring a smile. After bemoaning having to sell his general stamp collection in order to do research in Europe, he ruefully noted:

> I am trying to force myself to ignore stamps and stick to my writing projects. . . . It's a quiet year, 1,400 students. Few very vocal. Agitation goes in cycles, I think. Faculty is sort of different too. I keep busy, 100 majors. . . . Regards to the

Gracious Stabilizer of the Wheeler household.
—Card of November 22, 1965

On hearing of our moving east to teach in an Alabama college, he wrote:

Happy to hear the news. I hope that this will prove a rewarding experience. I don't think there's any doubt that it will be fraught with interest. We will be watching the *Review* for later indications of your movements, upward and/or sideways. But in that climate, what will happen to mint stamps?
—Card of May 16, 1968

Through the years, I had bombarded him with an embarrassingly large number of requests for recommendations. Now, I had asked him for another:

The letter has been mailed. I hope it helps. I dislike these wide open requests for recommendation where you have to guess what they want but I suppose the checklist type is pretty useless too.

Thanks for the invitation to stop by Huntsville. I'll fly to NY then to Luxemburg and then bus to Paris, saving the school $70 or so and costing me an extra day and two nights sleep, but I have this old-fashioned compulsion about thrift and never having been an administrator, have never outgrown it in my limited travels.

Six months seem hardly time enough to grind through the mass of material I ought to check but I should at least touch the required bases before beginning to write. It is hard to

disprove a negative, and research is the same way. You can
never be sure that something does not exist and may pop up
to call a question on the data you have accumulated. Well,
there is no security anywhere in this world, I guess.
—An interoffice memo, February 5, 1969

Responding to grapevine accounts having to do with the college
in the Southwest where I was then teaching, he chortled:

We hear strange reports . . . about the wondrous ways your
educational leaders perform their wonders, as in selecting
presidents for your school. We surely have our problems too,
99 percent unnecessary, but I'm not sure I'd want to trade.
—Typed letter of April 15, 1971

One of my classmates, Dr. Bruce Anderson (in his "Not Some
Saintly Mr. Chips: A Memoir of Walter Utt," in *Spectrum*, vol.
18, no. 4), remembered Utt's impact on *his* life:

I realized when he died in 1985 that my file of 72 Utt
letters was one of my most precious possessions, the kind
you grab first when the house is on fire. I also recognized
that outside my immediate family, this Christian teacher had
been the most important person in my life.

Noting that some conservative church reactionaries considered
Utt to be a cynic, Anderson countered with

At heart he was a defender of the faith—witty, skeptical,
independent—but a defender nonetheless. Somebody once
said that the world is divided into two camps: liberals who

wonder why the world isn't better and conservatives who are surprised that it isn't worse. By that definition, Walter was a profound conservative.

All these thoughts and more sifted through the chambers of my mind during that day-long drive north to Pacific Union College. Then came the evening we all gathered in Dr. Utt's old classroom. His favorite cartoons and sayings still graced the walls. Cartoons such as the one by Baloo in which one caveman solemnly informs the other, "Do you realize that there are enough rocks to kill every man, woman, and child on earth five times over?" or another by Hector Breele depicting an impoverished man and woman sitting in a bare tenement flat, and she deadpans, "I sometimes find it hard to believe what it was like before we had nuclear power." And sayings or quotes such as,

Stupidity is actually responsible for much of what we attribute to malice.
—Anonymous

He leaps purposefully from fragmentary data to shaky assumption and on to firm conclusion.
—Book review in *American Historical Review*

Is the world run by smart ones who are putting us on, or by imbeciles who really mean it?
—Anonymous

A fanatic is a person who does what God would do if He had all the facts.
—Anonymous

> The spectacle of nuts seeking rendezvous with nutcrackers
> is not a pageant of the past.
> —Eliot Janeway

Gradually, as we chuckled at these tangible representations of his teaching life, the room filled. Some I knew from years before; many were younger than I and were unknown to me. The Utt family was there, as were a number of Utt's close friends among the faculty. Brooding over the room was an air of expectancy: *What was going to happen?*

Finally, the moderator stood, welcomed us, and stated that there was no program, no agenda: the program was *us*. Whatever we cared to say about this man's life—well, here was our opportunity to do so.

There was a long silence. If memory serves me right, I was either the first, or one of the first, to speak. I told them about all the letters and cards Dr. Utt had written to me since college, how all through the years, he had *been there* for me. I was more than a bit proud; I didn't say, but implied: *I must be someone very special.* Imagine my chagrin as I then listened to testimonial after testimonial and discovered that I was in a *room full* of men and women Dr. Utt had cared enough about to stay in touch with, to *be there* for, through the years!

I believe that experience was one of the defining moments of my lifetime—the revelation that I was anything but unique in Dr. Utt's life: merely one of *many!* That evening represents an epiphany in my life. It was the last domino of a cascade started several years before by an adult-degree student who asked me a most pointed question: "Dr. Wheeler, are you my friend just until graduation—or are you my friend for the *long haul?*" She knew I'd be there for her until graduation, for I was paid to be; but she wanted *more:* a friendship that would keep going after the money stopped. That question has gnawed at me ever since. Now, here in this old classroom was the memory of a *real* mentor, not a pale imitation of one. We are, after all, a society of throw-away relationships: *I'll be your friend for as long as the good times last, for as long as it's to my advantage to stay friends—but don't expect me to stay a moment longer!* Sadly, too many of our "friendships" are little better than one-night stands and are based on nothing but self-gratification.

So it was that it all came together for me: the past, the present, and the future. What was my response to be? After a great deal of soul-searching and prayer, I made a vow to God that from that day forward, the number-one priority for the rest of my life would be long-term, for-life, mentoring. Not just with students in formal classrooms, but with *everyone* the good Lord brought into my life. So many of these relationships are short, only moments long. I may sit next to someone in a plane, a train, a restaurant, a public gathering, and most likely will never see that person again—sort of like Christ's meeting the dissolute woman of Samaria at the well (we have no record that they ever met again). Same with the rich young ruler. Yet those two meetings have influenced men and women everywhere for almost two thousand years. After I made that solemn vow, the Lord led me back to the formal classroom for ten more years, then out of it again into the much broader classroom represented by my books, audiotapes, and day-to-day interactions with His sheep everywhere I go.

This is perhaps the greatest legacy I received from Dr. Utt. That and his belief in me, that God had a plan for my life—a mission, if you please, a responsibility uniquely mine.

Today there is a Walter C. Utt endowed Chair of History at

Pacific Union College, but the real Utt endowment is in our hearts and cannot possibly be measured in mere money.

So it is, will ever be, that the echoes of those shuffling footsteps and staccato taps of his cane, daily bring home to me this message:

Life is short, life is frail, and there is no guarantee of a tomorrow. All we have is today, this moment, and the people who come our way. In the end, our money, things, houses, and land will be passed on to others. The only thing that will remain to show that we lived on this earth will be the impact of our life, acts, and words on those whose lives intersected with ours.

And in years to come, may it be said of you, of me, by those who knew us and feel blessed:

"I can see him . . ."

"I can see her . . ."

If these stories of friendship touched your heart, you will enjoy Joe Wheeler's other collections of timeless stories:

HEART TO HEART STORIES OF LOVE

Representing several different eras and cultures and depicting love at various stages of life, this collection of stories is all about the different ways that love can be shown. From the tale of an army lieutenant's test of faithfulness to the story of an old Victorian rocking chair with a secret, this collection is sure to touch your soul as you enjoy the stories time and again.
0-8423-1833-X Hardcover (available July 2000)

HEART TO HEART STORIES FOR MOMS

This heartwarming collection includes stories about the selfless love of mothers, stepmothers, surrogate mothers, and mentors. Moms in all stages of life will cherish stories that parallel their own, from those showing how a child's life can be touched by a woman's love to those demonstrating the bond between child, mother, and grandmother. A collection to cherish for years to come.
0-8423-3603-6 Hardcover (available March 2000)

HEART TO HEART STORIES FOR DADS

These classic tales are sure to tug at your heart and take up permanent residence in your memories. These stories about fathers, beloved teachers, mentors, pastors, and other father figures are suitable for reading aloud to the family or for enjoying alone for a cozy evening's entertainment.
0-8423-3634-6 Hardcover (available March 2000)

CHRISTMAS IN MY HEART
Volume VIII

These stories will turn hearts to what Christmas—
and life itself—is all about. Powerful and
inspirational, each story is beautifully illustrated
with classic engravings and woodcuts, making the
collection a wonderful gift for family members
and friends. Reading these stories will quickly
become a part of any family's Christmas tradition.
0-8423-3645-1 Softcover (available November 1999)